GOOD COP GRANDPOP

Donald P. Borchers
Chad Lutzke

Encyclopocalypse Publications
www.encyclopocalypse.com

GOOD COP GRANDPOP

ONE

MAXIMILIAN TYRELL PAYS no mind to the fireworks across the bay, exploding somewhere above the San Francisco Giants' Oracle Park. His focus is on the street and the houses where he's parked. It feels good to be sitting here, buried in the shadows, binoculars in hand. Like old times, something he doesn't realize how much he's missed, until now.

He sits behind the wheel of his Toyota Cressida inside an Emeryville, California gated community. The car is orange. Not exactly inconspicuous. But at least it's not a van. People question vans, particularly people with something to hide.

Max rubs at sixty years of living etched in his unshaven face, and the car fills with the subtle sound of grit, as his nails scratch the stubble on a jaw reaching senior years. He stops, squints. The passenger riding shotgun, quiet as a dead mouse.

"See those security cameras and motion detectors over there?" He points toward a house with black shutters, its front door painted a brick-red. "In plain sight, right?" The coffee in his hand finds his mouth, and he takes a sip. "But, all that expense is worthless if you got a pro. By the looks of things, we got a real pro workin' here. I've trained more than my share of rookies, and, trust me on this, the big mistake they all make is not following the rules. *My* rules. By the letter. And that's what gets 'em killed. Now, it looks like we're going to be together for a long time, Cadet, so we need to get a couple of things straight, right up front. One: No drinking without a lid on your cup, for fast breakaways." He proudly holds his cup for the silent passenger to take note of its secure lid. "And two: Stay alert. Don't sleep on the job. Keep an eye out for anything unusual. Anything at all."

The passenger—Talulah, a ten-year-old girl pulling from a straw tucked inside a juice box, looking out of a pair of kid's detective binoculars. "Like that?"

Startled by his granddaughter's find, Max pushes her head down slightly, keeping the two of them in stealth mode. He peeks above the dashboard and squints again.

Across the street, a shape moves from the shadows and through a pool of light. A cat. The slick feline passes under the motion detector and climbs the trellis, its every move like some old routine. It brushes against the security camera, forcing the camera's view away from the front of the house. Then the cat jumps down to the front porch and barges into the house through the doggie door.

Max and his granddaughter watch intently from the car, waiting. She wiggles in her seat with anticipation, her auburn hair pulled back tight into a ponytail, a dull pink scrunchie holding it in place. The scrunchie is old and losing its elasticity, but it was her mother's, making it special. Max can't remember ever seeing his granddaughter without it. If it isn't in her hair, it's around her wrist.

He takes the moment in, captures it with his mind's eye and officially stamps it as a memory worth saving. For Talulah, the exciting stakeout is a well-needed escape from reality. For Max, it's much more—an important moment to share with the only person he has left, a chance to share who he is deep down, and a small taste of how he used to spend his days on the force.

Max turns to the tiny passenger and cracks a prideful smile at his cadet, as she watches silently for the cat's exit, wholly dedicated to the mission at hand. Max nearly misses seeing the cat himself, when the tabby walks back through the small door, a smartphone jutting from its mouth.

"Aww," the girl says, bright eyes still through the binocs. "A real cat burglar. Do you think he's a stray?"

Max takes another sip of coffee, puts his car in gear, and squints, eyeballing the cat. The Cressida pulls out, in pursuit of its prey. "No, Talulah. I think he's a thief."

TWO

INSIDE THE MANAGER'S office at Forest Hills Condominiums, down the street from the stakeout, Max holds out an open palm as the manager slips a signed check into it. Easy Money. A cat is no threat. Worst case? A few scratches. Never any chance of gunfire, fists to the face, or a baseball bat to the kneecaps.

The manager lets go of the check. "You need a referral, Max…" Pulls a toothpick from his mouth he'd been working a bit of pickle with, "…just ask."

Max nods, offers a tight-lipped grin that hides maybe too much pride for such a menial task, and squints at the check, looks it over.

The cat burglar sits in a cage on the counter, on display like a cheap attraction—a drive-through zoo that might sell swag reading: "I survived the cat burglar, and all I got was this lousy T-shirt."

Max points at the mewling thing. "Busy cat." He does a once-over of the cat's stolen hoard, sitting in a pile next to its tiny jail cell—the smartphone, a baseball glove, Porsche sunglasses, a Jimmy Choo shoe, and more.

The manager pulls the toothpick from his mouth and

waves a hand over the treasure trove of hot goods. "The owners of this stuff will be grateful."

Talulah puts a tiny finger through the cage and touches the striped orange and white fur of the cat's tail. The cat responds with a plaintive meow. This makes her smile, something that doesn't happen as often as it used to. "What will happen to him?"

The manager, very nonchalantly, and with the bedside manner of a toaster, says, "Being a stray, and considering his age, he'll most likely be put to sleep."

As though responding to the proposed death sentence, the cat meows again, and Talulah flashes wide eyes at Max, carrying with them the weight of the world. "If Mom were here, she'd rescue him."

The girl is right. Her mother would indeed rescue it. She'd rescue ten of them given the chance. Max recalls his daughter, Susan, bringing home a puppy when she was young. The neighbors had recently brought one home, and the pup had run away, making its way down the block, where Susan fell in love with its wagging tail, absolutely ready to sign up for a fifteen-plus-year commitment, promising to buy its food with her own money made from chores. Max nearly caved before being saved by the neighbor, when it was revealed they'd actually been looking for their missing dog after discovering a hole in the fence.

But cats? The idea was even less attractive, and so Max shakes his head before his retort begins. "No. No way. No how. Not going to happen. Not on my watch." the pleading eyes glass over as his words hit like bullets. "Not in my lifetime. Never in a million years."

But hell freezes, pigs fly, and within minutes, the cat walks out a free soul, having stolen once again, this time the heart of a ten-year-old girl and the once adamant stance of a stubborn man whose career these days is appeasing the girl.

THREE

MAX PARKS the Cressida in front of St. Jude's—one of the smallest Catholic churches in San Francisco but big enough to carry the burden of Max's own confessions through the years.

The cat—still without a name—jumps from the car after Max, a leash connecting them. The thin nylon rope is like a heavy chain, attached to the other end is the iron responsibility he'd rather not have, and the occasional resistant tug is a reminder the man isn't in control, not as much as he'd like to be. In his other hand is a shopping bag.

The church reminds Max of any dive bar in the middle of the day. Dark. Its own distinct smell. Quiet. A place for sinners.

He dips his fingers into the holy water, does the obligatory crossing and makes his way to the altar, bends a knee that feels like two grinding stones. If the crackling of the joint were any louder, it would echo.

He pushes off with a calloused hand on his knee, struggles to stand, then makes his way to the confessional. Darker still. Quieter. Another place for sinners.

There is no priest on the other side of the booth. Not

yet. Max reaches into the shopping bag and pulls out a sandwich wrapped in waxed paper. He peels the wrapper open, leans back, and takes a bite of fresh deli. The cat does half a circle at his feet before nestling in between his leg and the wall. Content, both of them.

Inside St. Jude's, a Hispanic woman in her forties kneels and lights a candle. Behind her, Father O'Brian—Irish blood, nearing retirement, if not there already—walks between the pews, slows to a stop as he hears the unmistakable sound of a snore coming from the nearest confessional. With an educated guess of who's inside, he shakes his head and sighs.

O'Brian opens the priestly side of the booth and taps the frosted glass between them. The snoring continues. The godly man then slams the confessional's door, and the cat springs to life on the other side, alongside Max, who quickly drops to his knees. The stones crackle and grind, and his teeth grit. Another ritualistic signing of the cross.

"Forgive me, Father, for I have sinned. It's been..." Max trails off, trying to recall just how long it's been.

Father O'Brian grabs the bridge of his nose, shuts his eyes tight. "Yesterday, Max. Sweet Mary, mother of God, your last confession was yesterday!"

The cat meows, as though adding its own two cents.

"Does your new friend have a name?" O'Brian says.

Max looks down at the cat and furrows his brow. "No. And we ain't friends."

"Okay... so, what is troubling you today, Max?"

"Well, for starters, my oversized prostate's driving me nuts."

Father O'Brian lets out another sigh, a familiar part of

his vernacular when in the presence of Maximillian Tyrell. "Stop being an asshole, Max. I'm not in the mood."

"Sorry, Father. I'm trying *really* hard to stop swearing. How's that?"

O'Brian rests the back of his head on the confession wall. "You need a hobby. Retirement has given you too much free time."

"I don't want your advice," Max says. "I want your absolution."

"We've talked about this, Max. To be forgiven, you must first learn to forgive."

Max shakes his head, looks at the dark ceiling, glares through it. "Twenty-six years ago, my ex-wife baked me an apple pie. My favorite dessert." He pauses, reflecting on the memory. "I came home from work, and she'd left me a note: 'Dear Max. I've met the love of my life, and I'm leaving you. Try not to choke on the pie.' Could you forgive that, Father? I mean... I can't even stand the sight of an apple these days."

"Yes, I could."

"Why?"

"Because I don't want to be like you. You're a walking time bomb. Pissed off at the world. Then you come in here every day asking for absolution. Let go of this pent-up anger, Max. Or it's going to kill you. Matter of fact, heading across the street and ordering a slice of Dotty's homemade would do you some good."

A sneer slithers across Max's face. "The gospel according to Father O'Brian, huh? Don't crucify me with your liberal ideologies. I already know the rules: A man works hard, saves his money, buys a small house, is faithful to his wife, raises his kids, goes to church on Sundays, keeps his family on the straight and narrow. The gospel according to *me*. Now, what's wrong with that?"

"Nothing. And how's that working out for you?"

The priest slams his panel shut, startling Max, and exits the booth, while the bitter man left inside stares at his own reflection in the glass, the dim light deepening the lines in his face, adding years. He squints, and the lines deepen still. He stands, ignoring the warning his knees require, as one of them pops—a declaration of disapproval at the sudden movement.

"Jesus H–!"

The priest's scolding voice echoes through the tiny church, drowning Max out, "Maaaax! Try Harder!"

FOUR

TALULAH WALKS out of her elementary school in North Beach, a small tribe of other ten-year-olds with her. Sasha and Adriana. They're gossiping and giggling about a twelve-year-old boy with peach fuzz on his lip, who stands talking to his own friends just a few yards away.

Adriana, with her jean shorts and backpack, hikes the bag onto her shoulder and sidles up to Talulah. "He's sooo cute."

"And he's shaving already." Sasha gently claws at imaginary stubble on her own face, strawberry-blonde pigtails bouncing.

Max strolls through the parking lot and toward the walkway at the front of the school, where buses sit waiting for their delicate cargo. The cat follows close behind, its leash swinging from its collar to Max's hand. Kids run past, chasing one another, spilling homework from hand-me-down books—the beautiful chaos of another school day conquered.

Max reaches the girls, tearing their focus away from the puberty-stricken boy, and now they ooh and ahh over the slick feline trailing behind him—perhaps the best opportunity to unload the thing he's had yet. "You want to adopt a cat, Sasha?"

The girl shakes her head, bends down and strokes the cat's back. "We have a dog."

Max offers the leash to the other girl. "How about you, Adriana?"

"Mom's allergic. What's his name?" She joins her friend in petting the cat, who seems to be enjoying the attention, pushing up into their palms and purring.

Talulah looks at her grandfather through slit eyes. "We're not allowed to name him. That would create... *attachment*."

Max glares back, holding his own—a game of stink-eye. No words between them, but plenty is said. What Talulah doesn't see behind his glare is the morsel of guilt buried within. He knows her pain, these past few days without her parents. That morsel will remain hidden, for reasons neither of them can fully understand. But for now, the cat burglar has got to find a home.

Max and his granddaughter park outside IKEA in Emeryville. They're here for a twin bed. The parking lot is filled with people carrying their loads. One man with a new bookshelf across his shoulder, toting the thing without a struggle. While another's arms are filled with too many boxes of various sizes, his stride carefully swift toward the backend of a pickup truck.

Once inside, Max and Talulah walk with the cat. The creature doesn't seem to mind being on the leash, regardless of the crowd. Then again, it's not your typical cat. Typical cats don't burglar.

Max shakes his head at the price tag on one of the beds,

praying Talulah doesn't show any interest in that particular one. "So, how was your first day back?"

Talulah runs her finger along a headboard, collects the dust, and wipes it on her pants. "Adriana got a training bra."

Max's eyebrows shoot up, then slide back down. He does his best to ignore the embarrassing topic and pats a mattress, testing it. He clocks the price tag, making sure it's within budget. The cat jumps onto it and plops down. "This one's pretty firm. And firm is important for your back. Trust me. Firm's what you look for."

Talulah tests the bed too, by flopping onto it. "I want a training bra." She spreads out, as though making a snow angel on the bare mattress, gently kicking her grandfather out of the way.

Max stands and pulls an old cigar from his shirt pocket, chews on it, considers the topic of bras and how his daughter would handle it. Or any woman for that matter. "Your mother thinks you're too young."

Talulah pulls in a deep breath, exhales. "You mean... *thought*."

The weight of the word crushes the man, and he wants nothing more than distraction. Another prayer answered, and a couple pass by, wrestling over a garish lamp in the man's hand.

"Grow up!" the woman says. "I'm not living in a college dorm."

"And I'm not living in a sorority house." The man's grip on the lamp tightens as he tugs it away from the woman's hands.

"No. We're living in your parents' basement. Get a job!" she says.

The couple are in their early twenties, but Max thinks they could be as young as nineteen. He struggles with guesstimations these days. Girls start wearing make-up—

and apparently bras—far too young, and the young men seem to be shaving by the time they hit high school.

Max studies the couple and pulls the cigar from his mouth. Talulah seems to sense what's coming next. "Stay out of it, Max." But he takes no heed and hands the leash to his granddaughter. "It's not worth it," she pleads.

With a determined stride, Max moves to the couple and steps between them so they're forced to end the bickering and acknowledge him. The man looks confused, shocked even. Max offers a quick flash of an SFPD badge in his wallet, pulls him to the side and looks him in the eye. Holding up a hand, Max says, "Wait here. And zip it."

In the meantime, Talulah sneaks away. She drops the cat's leash, rolls off the bed, and crouch-walks down the aisle toward IKEA's exit, past shelves filled with pillows and linens, keeping hidden from Max along the way.

Max turns from the man, steps toward the woman.

"Butt out, or I'll call a cop," she says. The fire in her eyes speaks volumes. This woman is serious and not to be trifled with.

Max holds out his SFPD retired officer badge, again. But he puts his forefinger over the word "Retired." "Easy, sweetheart. I *am* the law."

Call it instinct he's learned only the last few years, but something pokes at him, an itch that needs scratching, a nudge that can't be ignored.

An alarm that screams Talulah is gone.

He swivels his head toward the mattress. The instinct was right. She's gone. He runs to the empty mattress, as though getting closer would reveal something more. A clue. But even the cat is gone.

Max scans the store, his eyes landing on the closing front doors, catching the last bit of leash as it drags on the ground before it disappears. It's the only clue he needs. He bolts after.

Outside, he scans again. Left. Right. The sun is against him. His eyes take their time adapting to the contrast, and everything blurs. He makes a circle with a forefinger, puts a squinting eye to it—a makeshift pinhole telescope.

The tops of cars emit heat waves above them, like ghosts eager to find cooler air. A rogue shopping cart rolls across the lot, threatening to dent the first car it meets. Shoppers load their items into trunks, unload their kids from back-seats. Finally, across the parking lot, the cat comes into view, among a crowd of people who wait on the corner of a cross-walk, weaving in between their legs. The pedestrian light there blinks *DON'T WALK* as the cat perches under it, yawns, then proceeds to groom itself. Long, heavy licks with a spiked tongue.

Max puts the cigar back in his mouth and makes a determined dash toward the corner. His knee shows grace, and he makes good time, but when he reaches the crosswalk and lunges for the leash, the light changes, and the cat is lost in the crowd.

It suddenly occurs to Max the cat could be leading him on a wild goose chase. What if it's not following Talulah at all? Maybe she went one way and the fur-ball another. Doesn't matter. For now, it's the best lead he's got.

Max's eyes dart about, looking for the cat. Finally, he spots its swift movement, slithering between a hundred legs. Max breaks into a full sprint, ignoring the creeping pain in his knee, and runs half a block before the cat dips into the open door of a storefront. Victoria's Secret. The little perp is really pushing his buttons.

There are some stores a man can go his whole life not stepping foot in. For Max, that'd be pet stores, jewelry stores, and Victoria Secrets.

He and his aching knee arrive at the door and head in, stopping just inside to scan the place. He wipes sweat from his brow downs a gulp of air. A sweaty, old man out of breath, standing in a sea of lace and silk. It doesn't look good.

Max looks out over the sea. Black, white, pink, and red waves. Women holding teddies up to their chest in front of mirrors, testing the waistbands of panties that will barely cover their goods. One woman, fresh from the changing room, has her shirt off and is covered only by silky C-cups, picking out a different bra on the discount rack to try on.

Finally, Max spots someone who isn't busy with lingerie—a sales clerk in her thirties with "La-a" on her name-tag stands near a rack of sheer, black bras. He jogs up to her. "Excuse me, "La, Ah? You seen–?"

"It's Ladasha." The woman points to the pink name-tag on her chest. "La...dash...a." She looks Max up and down, sees the agitation in his face, mistakes the red in his cheeks for an embarrassing blush, and a lightbulb seems to go off in her head. "Oh, don't worry, honey. Your secret's safe with Ladasha."

Max doesn't get it. His focus is on the cat, dead-set on finding the thing before it walks out with a garter in its mouth. He squats down, looks under bins, counters, racks.

Nothing.

He stands, knee popping, and comes face to face with the clerk. She's holding a dress with a plunging neckline, bra, and panties. He takes a step back, and she takes one forward, measuring him up with her eyes.

"Extra-large, bust size... about 38A." She drapes the yellow dress across his chest. "See? This color does wonders for your complexion."

Max gently grabs her arms and moves her aside, his eyes frantically searching the sea behind her. The woman, oblivious to Max's real desire, carries on with her pitch. "And I've got the perfect shoes for this outfit. What are you...?" She looks down at his feet. "Size fourteen? We can get those." She takes a step, moving back in front of Max and revealing Talulah behind her at the checkout, cradling the cat.

Max storms over to his granddaughter, fire in his eyes. "Tryin' to give me a heart attack?"

Talulah shakes her head and defends herself. "You went full hashtag *control-freak* back there. I thought I'd be back before you even noticed."

"Oh, I noticed." He pauses, realizing she's actually in line with the intent to purchase something from this sinner's den. "What are you trying to hide from your old grandfather here?"

Talulah slips her hand behind her back. "Mind your business."

With a speed that impresses them both, he snatches the white silk from her hand. It's a training bra. Heads swivel toward Max and his granddaughter, and the half-naked woman ducks back into the dressing room with a handful of bras.

"Max! Stop treating me like a child." Talulah stomps her foot on the tile floor.

"You're ten *hashtag* years old!"

Talulah's mouth opens, then freezes there. Her eyes widen and well with tears. Max reaches out, puts a hand on her shoulder and gives it a firm but gentle squeeze, one that says he's here. Always. That he knows how rough it's been. None of this has been easy. He knows that. But she steps out of reach and wipes her eyes.

"I miss Mom and Dad," she says, chin quivering.

Max looks at the floor, feeling defeated by the young child's mournful eyes. "So do I, Cadet."

Talulah sniffs the grief back and redirects with a single, random statement. "You should name the cat."

Max can't tell if this is manipulation or, more likely, a desperate attempt at swaying from a very touchy subject. He lets the words hang in the air, until he feels Ladasha brush against him. She leans into his ear. "If now's not a good time, check back tomorrow. We're having a sale."

FIVE

THE MOON SHINES down on a San Francisco neighborhood, spotlighting expertly trimmed lawns and beautiful, lush gardens. And then there's Max's house, the wart in the middle of this gentrified hilltop district. The hangnail among the manicured. At the very least, it could use a paint job, perhaps a sprinkler to bring some color to the patchy lawn. It was never this bad, but sometime after his wife ran off and left him, the neglect started, and now even the bugs keep to the other side of the street.

Inside the house, Max chews his cigar—a necessary break after putting together Talulah's new bed from IKEA. He reflects on the proud moment of a job well done. The bed stands sturdy in the far corner of her room. Hopefully, this is the first step in making his home feel like hers.

Talulah walks in with a glass of prune juice, hands it to her grandfather, while the cat takes the IKEA assembly instructions in its mouth.

Max takes the juice. "Thanks. But still no training bra." He pulls the unlit cigar from his teeth and plops down on the new bed. It collapses under him, and a splash of juice hits his shirt. Talulah giggles, and it's almost good, even under the circumstances. Just to see his little Angel smile these days is something special.

"I want to go see your favorite person," she says, ruining an otherwise fine moment. Max knows where this is going and huffs dramatically, wiping juice from his shirt.

"I said I want to—"

"I heard you." He pushes off the crumpled bed, being careful not to spill more juice.

"I love him, and I want *us* to see him."

"Who?" Playing coy, the old man takes a sip of juice. The glass hides his curling lip.

"Stop going all convict on me."

Max's attention is drawn to the cat, watching him, nestled on the floor with the instructions still in its mouth and chewing on them. He looks back at his granddaughter. "Let me make this clear. I'd rather croak than see Doyle Donovan again. Copy that? And what makes you think he'd even talk to me, anyway?"

"Why *wouldn't* he talk to you?" The words are barely out of Talulah's mouth before a lightbulb goes off. "Oh yeah. Because the last time you saw him, you made him cry."

Max puts the cigar in his pocket. "I did not *make* him cry. He *chose* to cry. And he's a dirty, rotten, lowdown, thieving scoundrel."

"Say that again, and I'll poison your prune juice." Talulah nods toward the glass in his hand.

Max glares through squinted eyes. "You don't scare me."

Talulah spots a few extra screws on the floor that belong in the bed. She picks them up and hands them to her grandpa. "Forgive and forget, Max."

"I have a real problem with that. *And* that burned-out grifter."

"Then deal with it! He's my grandpop. Just like you."

"Doyle Donovan is nothing like me."

"You're right. Because he's the sweetest, kindest, most thoughtful, loving, and caring person in the world." Talulah bursts into tears and runs from the room, slamming the door behind her.

Max stares at the closed door and the frame around it, the frame littered with black marks where countless times he stood Talulah's mother there and recorded her height, each scribbled line one step closer to the woman she would become. One step further from being daddy's little girl. Some of the lines are thicker than others, declaring a sense of excitement at a new milestone. Four feet. Five feet, and even senior year, the last day of school, when the young woman reluctantly gave into her father's persistence on measuring just one more time. Five feet, seven inches. He can't be sure, but he suspects she may have grown an inch since then. Now he wishes he knew just how tall she was before she was no longer his. No longer here at all.

The mental file of pleasant memories isn't large enough for Max to find solace in, not when his daughter has gone this soon, the prime of her life. If anyone should be gone it should be Max. Cigars, the occasional booze-filled binge, a strict diet of fried foods, and life as a cop for the SFPD is enough to knock at least a few decades off an average lifespan.

Max goes to the frame and runs his finger across the last line at the top. "I really wish you were still here, Princess."

The cat brings Max the partially chewed assembly instructions. Max snatches them out of cat's mouth, "What's your angle?"

SIX

PARADISE VILLAGE—AN upscale assisted-living community that's home to a multitude of active senior citizens located on the outskirts of the city. All four stories plastered with ceiling-high windows, providing a pleasant aesthetic both inside and out. The building itself is only ten years old, built by a San Francisco "old money" heiress who discovered aging is scarier than anticipated. This drove her to provide an escape from this reality for others, because not everyone has an inheritance to help pay for their million-dollar home, so why not offer rooms that feel like they're nestled in one.

Doyle Donovan, a striking figure of a man, mid-to-late-50's, stands in one of these rooms—the home of elderly resident, Lydia Scarfoli. The empty champagne bottle in his hand and the ever-present twinkle in his eye says he's up to no good. Doyle has naturally tanned skin, in stark contrast to the white suit he wears. His hair still holds the brown from younger years. Still full, with no threat of thinning. His dark eyes can turn from sympathetic to stern with a twitch of his brow, and his teeth all accounted for, save for the bicuspid he lost in a fight with a bookie, and a molar he lost to his love for lemon drops.

"You, my passion flower," he says, "are tantalizing beyond words." He takes the framed photo of a husband and wife from the nightstand and lays it face down.

Lydia, the woman in the photo, now much older, sits on the bed, batting her eyes thick with mascara. She has healthy hair for a woman her age, pulled up into a messy, graying bun, a long curl threatening to hide the side of her face. She holds a pen in one hand, a checkbook in the other. "Che bello! You make my heart go pitter-pat."

Doyle takes her hand, kisses it, sees a large diamond resting atop her ring finger. "And... Mr. Scarfoli?"

"Had an unfortunate heart attack."

"I am deeply sorry." Another kiss to the hand that smells of lavender. "My condolences."

Lydia turns her head, and the curl bounces. She rolls her eyes. "Oh, please. He died in the saddle. And it *wasn't* mine."

Doyle looks into her eyes, squints. "Can you keep a secret?"

"I'll lock it away in a very safe place, where I keep my age." She winks, and the crow's feet at her blue-gray eyes whisper the age of sixty-eight, give or take a few years.

"Rumor is, the Nobel Committee is considering the fund." He holds a finger to his lips. "Now, mum's the word."

"Magari! Oh, I forget..." Lydia clicks her pen with excitement and places the tip on a blank check. "...what's the name of that divine charity of yours?"

"Care and Save Humanity."

The aging woman nods, looking at the check she's written for one thousand dollars. "Oh dear. I don't think I can fit all of that on here."

Doyle strokes the woman's shoulder with a smile. "Just use the initials, love."

Like a grade-school child, the woman recites each letter as she writes it, drawing the syllables out. "C-A-S-H." She hands Doyle the check, as well as a stack of neatly folded clothes, then heads for the bathroom. She leaves the door ajar while she disrobes, then tosses her clothes over the door. "Una picolla memento."

"And not an instant longer," Doyle says, busy with the switch of his own wardrobe. It takes him all of sixty seconds to don the purple cap and gown she'd provided. He looks at himself in the mirror and shakes his head, then looks at the check, as if to say "It's all for you, baby." He drops into the chair behind him and reclines, sipping his mimosa, gazing at the check, and savoring the moment.

"Ready or not, here I come," Lydia says from bathroom, her voice filled with seduction.

Doyle pockets the check. "I'm quivering with anticipation."

"But first, I've something to confess, sir," she says. The bathroom door squeaks open further and out steps Lydia, sporting a blonde wig, plaid skirt, white cotton top, knee socks, and saddle shoes. She hooks a finger in her mouth and offers an innocent pout. "I've been a bad girl." She bats her lashes. "A very, very bad, little schoolgirl." She swings a hip out, extends a leg. It's not the first time she's played this role. "I lost my homework. Please, forgive me, Professor."

Doyle smiles, takes in the sight before him. "There's a punishment for naughty little schoolgirls like you." He sits upright in the chair, awaiting her arrival.

"Do they get a proper spanking?!"

Doyle only nods. No words.

"But I have an excuse, Sir. A very good excuse." She glides closer to him. "Oh, please don't spank me, Sir. Please don't–" She hikes her skirt up, revealing white cotton panties. "–spank me." This isn't the body of your average woman approaching seventy. This is years of hard work by a woman who refuses to let age take her without a fight. And of course, some parts were provided by the surgically precise–as well as expensive–hands of her celebrity plastic surgeon.

Another swing of her hips, and she's to the chair. She bends down carefully, places one knee at a time on the floor, and lies across Doyle's lap. "...Please!"

Doyle gulps the last of his mimosa and sets the glass down, before giving Mrs. Scarfoli's behind a playful slap.

Lydia's eyes go wide. "Oh, my! Professor!"

Doyle rolls his eyes and goes for another slap, when the door bursts open.

Emma Schlumburger rushes in—a woman older than Lydia, and looking older than her actual age, wearing a stylish hat, veil, and feather boa. She brings her matching purse up high and brings it down on Lydia's behind, batting at her with the designer bag. "Lydia! You man-stealing tramp! You stole my turn, you slut!"

Lydia swings around and takes purchase of the pink boa, yanking it. Emma whirls on unsteady, high-heeled feet and nearly falls.

Doyle slides between the two, separating the combatants and stopping the purse from connecting again. His cap falls off in the struggle, but he manages to get Lydia to release her grip. "Ladies, ladies! Please."

Emma clutches her purse and reaches inside, pulls out a small appointment book covered in a collage of brightly-colored flowers. She points at it with a chicken-bone finger. "It's in my book. Eleven PM! *An Affair to Remember*. Right here!"

Doyle cranks his neck and examines the entry in

Emma's address book. "No, Emma. That says *tomorrow* night."

Emma covers her gaping mouth, and her brow bends with embarrassment. "Oh my. I'm sorry, Lydia." She places a wrinkled hand on her friend's forearm. "Please forgive me. I don't have senior *moments*. I have senior *hours*."

"Non te la prendere. Did you check your blood sugar this morning?"

"No. That must be it. Thank you, darling." Emma drops the appointment book back into her purse.

Lydia waves the misunderstanding away and spots her friend's shoes. "Love your shoes. Are they new?"

Emma smiles and looks down. "Indeed." She pulls the boa close to her, as the feathers tickle her face. And just like that, all is forgiven, as the conversation switches from man-stealing whores to the discomfort of heels and how they're just not worth it anymore.

SEVEN

IN HIS DARKENED BEDROOM, Max wears white boxers and a T-shirt he's had for nearly forty years, baring the faded remnants of a transfer that once read *As Little As Possible.* He lay stretched out and snoring atop cotton sheets, the fitted one sporting a nine-inch tear near the corner, where he tugged it violently out of frustration two years ago.

The cat pounces on his head, and his eyes snap open. He squints at the clock. It's 4:30 AM. The alarm is set for 5:00 AM. He groans, reaches out to the nightstand and turns on the lamp, farts. The air pollutes with a sulfuric odor not unlike an egg that'd been left in the sun since the Clinton administration.

He sits on the edge of the bed and begins the morning ritual, first donning his knee brace, then the ACE bandage around his elbow. He stands and very slowly stretches his aching muscles. Involuntary grunts escape as he painfully moves to circulate blood. Gently pivoting his body, he swings his arms. After the usual pops and crackles, he slips on a pair of sweatpants and sits back down. Tying his running shoes takes more out of him than anything else, and the grunts grow in volume as he gets the job done. It just may be time for some slip-ons. Velcro? Hell no. But a pair of Skechers could do the job.

When the ritual is done, he stands in front of the mirror and sees the cat staring back, its front legs tucked under itself. "What are you looking at?" Max grabs his wallet off the dresser and pockets it, then grabs his handgun and leaves the bedroom. The cat follows.

In the kitchen, the walls could use a rehaul. The retro flowery pattern has been tainted yellow by years of cigar smoke, toning down the bright colors, but the dulling makes it no more appealing than if it held its natural loudness.

Max flips on the kitchen light and opens the cupboard. Except for a box of bran flakes, bottle of aspirin, and a container of Metamucil, the cabinet is bare. He grabs the aspirin and shakes a few out. The fridge doesn't hold much more: Coffee, beer, leftovers, prune juice, and a couple cartons of .38 bullets.

Behind him, the cat laps up the last of the milk from a bowl, while Max washes down the aspirin with the prune juice, killing two birds. Ease the pain and keep the stool motivated.

He peeks into Talulah's room and watches her sleep long enough to have a smile threaten his stone face. He looks around the room. There's nothing here to show it's inhabited at all, let alone by a ten-year-old girl. The walls are bare. No hanging fairy lights. No stuffed animals littering the bed. No posters of musical idols or Hollywood hunks and starlets. Just a single picture of her parents on the nightstand, facing her bed, as though she might like to think she's being watched by them, like guardian angels.

Max makes a note to spruce the room up and do what he can to make it feel like home. In the meantime, he heads outside for an early-morning run, rolls the trashcans to the curb, ignores the note written in dust on the Cressida: "Mow your lawn, asshole!"

The cat follows him, dragging the attached leash on the ground. It does well on a leash, not like most cats, who throw themselves on the ground with all the melodrama of a silent film star.

Next door, eighty two-year-old Norm Purvis mows his lawn, despite the sun barely offering enough morning light to do so. Norm has lived there for as long as Max can remember. Generations have poured from that house over the years, left the nest, then brought their own brood back for holiday visits. All in all, Norm is a decent neighbor and keeps to himself. Could stand to turn the TV down some in the summer months when the windows are open, but other than that, ideal.

"Hey, Norm." Max waves at him. "Don't forget trash collection."

The elderly man waves back and tilts his head. "Rash protection, you say?"

"Trash collection!"

"Can't hear ya. Hold on." The man does a shuffle with slippered feet and turns off the mower. "Say again?"

"The garbage man." Max points to his own trashcans on the curb.

"Huh? Oh, Hold on... hold on." Norm puts his hands up—a bundle of bony twigs wrapped in nicotine-stained parchment—then reaches into his pocket and pulls out two hearing aids, puts them in his ears, shakes his head. "Can't hear a thing without these. Now, what'd you say, Max?"

"Take your trash out, Norm. Today's pickup."

Norm raises a gnarled hand, lowers his head as if to concede. "I'm on it. Thanks for the reminder."

"Bye, Norm."

"Bye, Max."

Norm pockets his hearing aids and restarts the antique mower, while Max jogs away, enduring the pain as his knee cracks. The cat trots just behind, and the sun slowly paints the rooftops orange as day breaks on the Eastern horizon.

Drenched in sweat, Max and the cat wearily head into the house and walk down the short hallway. Talulah's bedroom door is open. He peeks inside, and his eyes are immediately drawn to the bare walls again. Maybe a few posters for starters. What is it these kids listen to these days anyway? Do they still like The Beatles? A Beatles poster would look great above that headboard. Sergeant Pepper could bring some color in here for sure. Or maybe one of those boy bands. Are those still a thing? He'll have to pay closer attention to what's written on her notebooks. Or do kids not do that anymore either?

He pushes the door wider to see the bed, and she's not there. In her place is a handwritten note resting on the pillow:

Dear Max,
    I'm meeting Grandpop at my old home. You're welcome to join us.
    Love,
    Your Cadet

Panic, frustration, a little bit of irritation knowing he's being forced to visit the enemy to get to Talulah. Doyle Donovan isn't exactly his idea of good company.

Max parks the Cressida outside his granddaughter's old apartment building. It's the last place he wants to be. He and the cat walk to the directory, a walk that twists his gut a little more with each step toward the door.

Max pushes the buzzer. No answer. He tries the door. It's locked. Moments later, a young woman exits, and Max catches the door with his foot. She sees the unlawful entry and throws her hands on her hips. Her face goes sour, none too happy a strange man thinks he's going to pull that trick.

"Do you live here?" she says.

Without a word, Max flashes his retired SFPD badge.

But this woman has keener eyes than he's used to and points out the problem with his credentials. "That badge says 'retired'."

Max pockets the badge. "Don't get your panties in a twist, missy. My granddaughter lives here." He turns around and heads inside.

"Well, then you should ring the appropriate–" And the door shuts, as the woman's muffled voice becomes a distant buzzing fly.

Max heads for the elevator as the doors of it slide open. Two women in their twenties are inside, mid conversation. "I want a result that looks natural, not 'done'," one of them says. "Dr. Webster showed me pictures of his work and made me feel confident about the procedure."

Max steps aside, smiles, and waves them out with a bow. One of the women offers him a wink.

"Dr. Webster is amazing. He did mine. Just look at them." the other woman says, then pulls down her tube-top and shows off the good doctor's work proudly.

Her friend cups each breast as if choosing a ripe melon at the market, then looks to Max. "What do you think? Should I go D or double D?"

Max steps into the elevator, and the doors begin to close. "C," Max declares with confidence, "... is the new D."

Any other day, and the encounter may have brightened his day. He may have even used the cat as a wingman, an excuse to linger a bit longer. Women love cats. But knowing the next face he sees will be the toothy grin of Doyle Donovon kills any chance of joy.

Thirty seconds later and the elevator dings. Max steps out onto the fourth floor and walks down the hall with the cat on its leash, heading for Talulah's old apartment, where she lived with her parents before life took an ugly turn.

He knocks on the door, hoping it's his granddaughter who answers and not the adversary–grandfather #2, a man Max could go the rest of his life never laying eyes on again. But the door opens, and there he is, teeth and all. Doyle has Max's hand in his, shaking it, before Max has a chance to recoil and curl his lip.

"Max. You look... how shall I put it? ...old."

Finally, that curl of the lip, and he pulls his hand away. "There's two kinds of people in this world," Max says. "And you ain't either one." His glaring eyes swing to Talulah, who sits on the couch, looking innocent. "You are on probation, Cadet."

She hops up and reaches for the leash in Max's hand. "Chill out, Max. Now... I'm going to feed the cat." She extends a scolding finger. "Promise you'll be extra nice to Grandpop." She takes the cat in her arms, nuzzles its neck, and heads for the kitchen.

"Fat chance. Either *It* goes..." Max points a thumb at Doyle. "...or I go."

With a smirk that has Max seeing red, Donovan says, "Talulah calls me, 'Grandpop', and she calls you 'Max'. You really like those odds?" Doyle plops down on the couch. "What's your problem, anyway?"

Max cranes his neck, checks to see if Talulah is out of the room and not within earshot. "I don't have a problem. If my daughter wanted to live in sin with your hobo-on-wheels, good-for-nothing, future welfare-sucking, liberal bottom-feeder of a son, who's never had a steady job... well, that was her problem. But me? I've got no problem."

"Okay, Max. So, my Cosmo wasn't the man you envisioned for your Susan. But they'd have been married if you just gave your blessing. That's on you, Scrooge. So, cut my kid some slack."

"He was thirty six years old and still used a skateboard for transportation."

Doyle takes a breath, runs a hand through his thick hair. "Have you gone completely senile, Columbo? My son *designed* skateboards." He points to the skateboarding posters on the wall. Susan Tyrell's Wharton M.B.A. is proudly displayed in a frame next to them.

Max rolls his eyes. "Like you need a PhD to nail a pair of skates to a plank."

Talulah returns with a bowl of cat food and sets it on the floor between the arguing men. The cat dives in, purring loudly as it eats.

"Talulah," Doyle says. "Would you please tell your bonehead grandfather that your mother loved your father?"

Max guffaws. "That supposed to make me happy?"

"Nothing makes you happy, McNulty. Except, holding a grudge." Doyle stands up and walks behind the couch, too agitated now to sit still.

Max has had enough, too. He turns and heads for a desk near the hallway, starts rifling through the papers and files scattered atop it. Skateboard magazines, clipped articles regarding skateboards, a few utility bills, and they're poking out from under a flyer advertising a lawn-care service, Max finds a Partnership Agreement between Cosmo Donovan and Susan Tyrell.

Doyle watches him from across the room with a gaze that's more lost in thought than paying any mind to what Max is doing. "Hey..." The tone of his voice changes. "You're not buying this *overboard* crap, are ya?"

"Put a sock in it." Max picks up a magazine, flips through it.

Doyle starts to pace. "Personally, I don't believe it was an accident. Something's not right. Period. There's gotta be a reason—"

"Then you must be the reason," Puts the magazine back down.

Doyle stops, shakes his head. "Wanna hear a great story about you?"

"Sure."

"So do I."

Max looks at Doyle and raises an eyebrow. "I still carry a gun."

"Stop! Both of you!" Talulah interjects, clearly frustrated. It reminds Max of his daughter. She looks at him. "What if Grandpop is right?"

Doyle looks at Max, eyebrows raised, as if to say *listen to her*. "It makes no sense. '*Falling overboard*' just doesn't add up."

Max gets lost in Talulah's big, brown eyes. She shouldn't have to worry about stuff like this. She should be worried about pimples and homework and her first trainer bra, not whether someone out there intentionally hurt her parents. He hates the idea of her losing sleep over this, on top of the grief she's already going through. So, if there is any hint of foul play in regard to what happened on that cruise ship, it needs investigating.

"Okay, look," he says. "I'll call Delgado and ask him to

get the security tapes from the ship. But when I watch them, I won't be responsible for what happens next."

"You've got an anger management problem. Own it," Doyle says.

Max looks to Talulah. "Do you think I have a problem with anger?"

"Max, I'm ten years old," she says. "Talk to your priest about your problems. Not me."

The response slaps Max silent. He digs out two Prilosec from his pocket, pops them in his mouth, and stomps down the hall toward the bathroom. "I gotta pee."

EIGHT

THAT NIGHT, the silhouette of Max sits in a chair in the corner of Talulah's bedroom while she sleeps. His eyes are solemn. It's hard to know what he's thinking, as hiding his feelings is one thing Max does best.

He draws a deep sigh and takes solace in the moment, while the moonlight streams through Venetian blinds, casting a shadow-ladder across Talulah's face. The cat quietly purrs on the pillow next to her. This is how Max spent the first few weeks of his daughter Susan's life, watching over her as she slept in her crib, awestruck by her beauty, reveling in how surreal it was that he had a part in creating something so perfect. Déjà vu.

He reaches for the blinds, closes them, shading her eyes from the moonlight. Except for the red glow of 5:00 AM from the old alarm clock, the room is black. He looks at her one last time before leaving, reflecting on how fast life can change, then quietly shuts the bedroom door and heads for the garage.

In the garage, a heavy bag that's seen years of wear and tear hangs from the rafters toward the back. An old black and white poster of a boxer hangs on the wall, the top half ripped and missing. It could be anyone. Ali, Spinx, even De Niro. Max wraps his hands in Ace bandages, then come the boxing gloves. He does his best to bounce on his feet, being mindful of the knee. But his real power is in the throws he sends the heavy bag, hitting it with jabs and crosses—a well-needed therapy session. Anger-management. And there's a lot to work with, especially this past week.

For another fifteen minutes, he gives the bag a necessary beating.

◯

Covered in sweat, Max makes a bologna sandwich with cheese, wraps it up, and puts it in a brown paper bag with an apple and small bag of potato chips. He sets the bag next to a box of Talulah's favorite cereal and a bowl, with his notebook computer and a note that reads: "Catch an Uber to school. I'll pick you up."

With too much to do, he's out the door. First stop, a cup of joe.

◯

At North Beach Coffee Shop, Max sips from a full cup of black, his unlit cigar stub rolls on the table whenever he bumps it. Patrons in the shop mind their business, faces in laptops and phones. Quiet as a library. Tethered to Max, the cat sits at a table, lapping milk from its own mug.

Max squints at a yellow 3 x 5 index card. He turns it face down, looks up, contemplates, then mumbles a succession of letters under his breath. He flips the card back over and checks it, shakes his head in disappointment. This feels a lot like high school, and the memory certainly isn't what it once was.

36

Max's focus is broken when he hears someone shout his name. He looks up from the card and spots a familiar face. It's Ira, a man in his 70s, making his away across the shop in a motorized wheelchair. A tank of oxygen rides shotgun. "Heard about your daughter," he says through a thick wheeze. "Pretty messed up, brother. I'm sorry. Never took a cruise myself." He takes a pull from the oxygen mask. "You doin' okay?"

Max sets the card down, looks Ira over, deciding whether or not today is the day he shares what's really on his mind. "My prostate's a pain in the ass." He offers Ira the leash. "You want a cat?"

Ira throws a hand up. "I hate cats." Max knows for sure one reason why the man hates cats, and it involves an accident on a hot summer day with the wheelchair, a cat's tail, and the shriek heard for miles.

Ira reaches for Max's card and tries to get a peek at it. "You tryin' to memorize something?"

Max slaps his hand away. "Mind your own business."

"Coming from you, that's rich," he wheezes. Something catches his eye, and he does a double take at the line of people waiting to order their morning fix. "Hey, Max." He nods, eyes glued to a busty woman. "Catch the redhead. Two o'clock."

Max looks at the line, finds the redhead. "On the hunt for a new nurse, Ira?"

"Roger that. Check out the rack."

"Your pacemaker'll short circuit."

Ira takes a deep pull on the oxygen. "Yeah, but what a way to go. Six to five they're after market."

"Can't be. Look at the jiggle." Max says as he scans the woman through squinting eyes. "Too much makeup, platform shoes, short dress. *And* it's fifty degrees outside. She's a working girl."

"Reminds me of a prowler I rolled on back in '92. A redhead answered the door." Ira can't help but grin at the fond memory. "...naked."

"What'd you do?" Max asks.

"Well... what else was there to do at three in the morning? What would *you* do?" The grin widens and splits Ira's face. "You know what I did." Then quicker than it came, the grin leaves as he melts into the wheelchair. "I can't do it anymore."

In attempt to lift the old man's spirits, Max pulls out his phone and flips to the gallery. "Got some new pictures." He scrolls through pictures of Talulah at church, on a stakeout, on the pier, and his favorite, where she sits on a hill just past sunset, overlooking the Golden Gate Bridge. It's a profile shot Susan had taken, where Talulah is in deep thought. When Max looks at the picture, he sees a young girl with the world in her hands. A girl he knows will overcome every obstacle in her way, be it mid-terms, puppy love, and even grief. All the potential in the world sitting on that hill, looking across the bay. Just as he is now, Max smiles every time he sees the image.

Ira comments on the array of pictures Max displays. "If I spent this much time with my third wife we'd still be married." He takes out his own smartphone and shows it off. "Here. Check out my new toy. Automated Want and Warrant system."

Max looks at the phone and nods, then moves a thumb across his own phone's screen and shows Ira an app. "Got you beat. A tracking app." Max reaches deep into his pocket and pulls out a small black disc that resembles a lithium coin battery. "It can pinpoint this tiny GPS device. Same one Delgado uses." The cat snatches Ira's phone with a curved paw. Max yanks the phone back with impressive reflex and hands it to Ira. Ira wheezes through a a weak chuckle.

Max nods at the cat. "He's on supervised probation, and I'm the supervisor. Here." He stands up, hands the leash over to Ira. "Hold this. I gotta pee."

Ira looks at the leash with surprise, then takes it and wraps it around his hand.

"Could take a while," Max takes one last sip of coffee.

Ira exchanges looks with the cat, "Should I be scared?" then he wraps the leash around his hand a second time, just to be sure.

Max makes his way to the restroom, puts a hand on the door and looks back. "Just keep an eye on your wallet."

As Max disappears through the door, Ira calls after him , "You're coming back, right?"

NINE

MAX PARKS the Cressida outside the DMV, and exits with the cat—now a familiar routine. They walk past a man sitting on the curb in a pair of sunglasses, holding a white mobility cane. A dog wearing a red vest with the words "Service Dog" across it lies near him. At the man's feet is a donation tin, which holds a few bills and some change. Max feels for the spare change in his pocket, and a sign above the DMV's front entrance catches his eye.

"NO PETS ALLOWED."

Max looks down at the dog, says to the blind man, "You gonna be here for an hour?"

The blind man nods.

"Wanna make twenty bucks?" Max pulls out his wallet.

Inside the DMV, people line the walls in chairs, holding small bits of paper with their number on it, waiting to be called. Most of them are on their phones, mindlessly passing the time. One woman does her waiting the old school way, with a copy of *People Magazine*.

Max enters the building with the cat in his arms. A few heads look up from their phones and watch him take a seat with the cat, which is now wrapped in the service dog's vest and fitting about as well as a grown man's blazer on a toddler.

For the next hour, Max studies the same index card he toiled over with his coffee–the sequenced letters of an eye chart. The cat watches him, seemingly entertained by the occasional sigh of disappointment whenever Max guesses wrong in this memorization game.

Max's number finally flashes on the screen behind the counter. He pockets the card, heads to window #7, and hands the appropriate papers to the clerk—a woman in her forties, whose reading glasses must only be for show, because not once has she put them on in the last hour, Max has noted.

"Do you wear glasses?" the clerk asks.

"Do I look like I need glasses?"

The cat looks up at Max, as though prepared to answer the question itself.

"Step over there." The clerk points toward the glorified ViewMaster that sits on another counter. A stick across the top reads Optec 1000 in bold letters. Sounds dated. Looks dated. "Put your head in the machine... You're going to read several rows of letters."

Max heads over and sets the cat down on the counter, then puts his face up to the contraption. The cat slips out of the service vest and brushes up against the Optec 1000, then looks at Max and starts plotting. As cats do.

"E, F, P, T...O, Z...L, P, E...D, P, E..." Max recites the letters he's been studying, much too concerned with their correct order to notice the cat now sniffing around his shirt pocket, then plucking the index card out.

C, F, D...E, D, F...C, Z...P...F, E, L." He pulls his smug face from the vision test machine. "How'd I do?"

The clerk looks at him sideways. "Haven't turned it on yet."

The cat walks over to the clerk with the card in its mouth and drops the cheat sheet in front of her.

Max has had experience with two cats his entire life. One was his neighbors calico, who had grown fond of the evergreen bush outside Max's front door, declaring it the ideal place to evacuate its bladder. Eventually, the ammonia-esque reek drifted through the open windows, so Max cut the bush down and poured cement in its place. His other experience involved an ex-girlfriend with a Siamese who racked up quite the vet bill–which Max was stuck paying–when the thing developed a habit of eating plastic wrappers, clogging its digestive tract every other month. So, Max has had no reason to love the furry things, and this klepto-narc with its tattling display just added to his list of complaints.

He and the cat trade looks. The cat's face is blank, could be a million different thoughts behind those eyes, but if the creature could extend a middle finger, Max thinks there'd be one showing. He shakes his head. "This is the thanks I get?"

○

Max sits in the Cressida, waiting for a gap in traffic so he can pull onto the four-lane road ahead. The road's as constipated as a wrapper-filled cat, cars moving at a snail's pace, while the klepto bathes itself in the backseat.

Meanwhile, Max watches a scene unfold.

A man in his thirties with slicked back hair, phone to his ear. He's in his own world, paying no mind, while his SUV and a subcompact car collide. The middle-aged woman driving the other car exits with an armful of paperwork pulled from the glovebox. Her hands are digging through her purse. She's visibly shaken.

The man hasn't moved. He's still on the phone, giving a play-by-play to whoever's on the other end. "Some brain-dead fool just swiped her little piece of junk into my baby."

Max knows this type. During the early years on the force, it was his favorite to issue a ticket to. Pompous. Pretentious. Absolutely self-absorbed. Oh, the apathetic souls he would crush with handing over a simple piece of paper. For the moment, he longed to be on the street again, sporting the uniform. This soul needed crushing.

The man finally gets out of his car, phone to ear.

"I think we're supposed to exchange information, sir?" The woman's voice cracks, offering all the appropriate info from her trembling hand.

"Hang on, dude," the man says to his phone. He turns to the woman. "Back off, bitch!"

Horns honk. The woman cries. And the sun beats down, turning the Cressida into an oven.

Max has had enough.

He grabs the cat off his lap, opens the car door, and gets out. He gives a leg a quick stretch, shakes it, and he's on the scene. "Okay, son. Get off the phone and give this nice woman your license, registration, and proof of insurance... as well as an apology."

"Suck butter from my ass, you old piss head."

Max smiles. Perhaps it's a way of burying the rage deep down, counting to ten, or thinking before he acts. Either way, his next move is lightning quick and precise, as Max rips the phone from the guy's ear, draws a pearl handled, .38 Smith & Wesson Hammerless Chief from its holster, and jams the barrel into the jittery man's throat. "Turn around. And spread 'em dirt bag."

Minutes later, lights flash, and the sound of sirens creeps its way to the accident as the sea of cars slowly parts, and more than one unit responds to the incident, one of them being SFPD Detective Lieutenant Hector Delgado.

The lieutenant steps from his patrol car. "Max, you can't call in and report 'man with a gun' when *you're* the man with the gun."

"Delgado... see the glassy eyes?" Max points at the man with the phone who started the mess. "Dilated pupils in daylight? He's under the influence. Hook and book the little snot-sniveling junkie."

"Hey, old man. I'm standing right here." Phone Guy says. "I'd like some respect."

Max reaches out and pats the man's shoulder. "And I'd like to be fifty again."

Through the side of his mouth, in a half whisper, Delgado orders Max to, "Put that away, right now," then throws an arm around him to hide the gun in Max's waistband. He shuffles Max off to the side of the road near a treeline. "Your badge is stamped 'retired' for a reason, brother. You're *retired*. So, stop being a cop and stop looking for redemption. For thirty-six years you did the right thing."

"Thirty-six *and a half* years. And I screwed up once. *One time*. And that's all they remember."

Among the chaos, the cat has found its way to Max and rubs against his leg, getting his attention. Max looks down and sees a leather wallet stuck in the cat's mouth. He quickly snatches the wallet, drops it on the ground, and kicks it under the car, then bends down and picks the cat up.

"What's with the cat?" Delgado says. "You hate cats."

Ignoring the man, Max looks at his watch. "I'm late. Catch ya later, Delgado."

TEN

MAX PARKS his Cressida outside Talulah's school, cat in his lap. He's late picking her up.

It's a picture of chaos at the school—buses being loaded, parents shuffling their kids into cars, some kids running, some standing around with gossip on their tongues. Max overhears a few of those as he walks briskly with the cat.

"Do you like him?" a girl with strawberry-blonde pigtails, every hair tightly pulled back. Max recognizes her as Sasha, one of Talulah's friends.

"He's sooo cute." Adriana, having traded her jean shorts for overalls.

Max interrupts them. "Where's Talulah?"

They shut their mouths and shake their heads, a message Max takes as suspicious.

◯

Max bursts into the principal's office pulling the two girls by their ears, the cat's leash stuffed into the palm of his hand. "These two are liars."

Looking up from his desk, the principal goes wide-eyed. "Max! You can't be serious!"

"My granddaughter is missing, and these little juvies are covering for her!" He tightens his grip on their lobes with the words, as they tilt their heads and wince in pain.

The principal stands, holding his hands up in a stance of submission and negotiation. "Now hold on. Let's put the pieces together here. Since you took her in, has Talulah wandered off on her own?"

"No. Never!"

The cat, licking its own paw, suddenly stops and cranes its neck at Max, making eye contact with a steely glare. The principal seems to notice.

Adriana pulls her ear away from Max's grip, and her curls bounce. "Talulah said she ran off a couple nights ago to Victoria's Secrets for a training bra."

Sasha speaks up. "And she told me that yesterday she snuck back to her old home to see her grandpop."

Max releases Sasha's ear and growls. He reaches into his jacket pocket and pulls out a foil sleeve of Prilosec. He pops a few out, tosses them back, and chews on them, as he stomps out of the office.

The next hour is spent questioning teachers, parents, administrators—any adult still on school grounds. Max even convinces the school to let him view the day's surveillance footage. He spends another half hour scanning, pausing, and rewinding the recorded footage for any clue as to where his granddaughter might be. Frustrated and furious, he jumps into his Cressida, guns the motor, and squeals off into an oncoming storm.

○

Rushing to the San Francisco Police Station, an impatient Max passes every slow-moving vehicle in front of him. He squints through the pouring rain, racking his brain, considering whether Talulah is just being rebellious or if there is truly something to worry about. Was this just another secret hunt for a training bra? Or was she in danger?

Deep in thought, Max passes the slow-moving vehicle ahead, squints, but still doesn't see an oncoming Trolley Car. Finally, he spots it in just enough time to swerve, nearly clipping it, avoiding a collision by a split second. With a racing heart, he pulls up to the curb in front of the San Francisco Police Station and parks in the red zone. Through a sheet of rain, he makes his way with the cat to the station, chomping a withering cigar. Soaking wet, he ignores the line of people inside and heads to the front.

Desk Sergeant Vogler points through the glass window between them to the NO SMOKING sign on the wall. Max rolls his eyes. "Seriously? It's not even lit... Where's Yablonski?"

Sergeant Vogler, surprisingly young for his position and not a hair out of place, says, "Don't know him."

Max pockets his cigar stub. "He's owned this shift since '96."

"Yeah, well, I'm the new guy." The sudden creasing in the man's brow ages him a few more years, adding a slightly harder edge to the clean-shaven baby face.

"I need to report a critical missing," Max says.

"Congratulations. But first, you need to wait in line." Vogler points again but this time toward the end of the line. Before Max has a chance to frown, the door buzzes, then opens, and a uniformed officer exits. Max whips out a chain lanyard, throws it around his own neck, and clips his retirement badge to it.

Before the door closes, he catches it.

"My granddaughter is missing," Max says. "And I need to see Delgado." He starts to move in through the door. "You probably don't know who I am. I'm retired."

"Guess again." The sergeant quickly steps to Max and puts a hand on his chest, pushing him back. The entry door closes. *Click!* "You had that thing back in '08 when you didn't wait for backup, right?"

"Thanks for the memory," Max says through the glass.

"Do we have a problem, Retired?" Vogler points again to the end of the line.

Max stomps past the people he attempted to cut in front of, offering the leash in his hand. "Anybody want a cat?"

After waiting in line, Max paces in Delgado's office. "Talulah always calls or leaves a note."

Delgado sits behind an old wooden desk, doing as little as possible. Picture frames, files, a nameplate, and a stapler that hasn't been used in years sits in front of him. "Did she say she witnessed anything?"

"Negative. Something's happened to her." Max stops pacing, lays eyes on the wall behind Delgado—a framed photo of himself and Delgado, their arms around a third cop.

"I need a list of her friends and relatives so I can run them down."

"I talked to her friends, and to the school. And I'm her only relative..." Max paces again. "...not counting Doyle Donovan." He struggles saying the name.

Delgado takes a long printout from his desk. "Well, Doyle's got a rap sheet I could sell on eBay. Busted seven times by the same detective..." Delgado glares at Max, and Max looks away sheepishly. "...and not one conviction. Sued the city each time for false arrest. Won the first lawsuit. Doesn't say how much. The others–"

"...were all settled out of court. Yeah, yeah. Get to the point."

The cat hops onto Delgado's desk, walks across it and lies down on top of the files, then rolls onto its back, feet in the air. The lieutenant rubs its stomach. "Word on the street is there's a few wise guys lookin' to tune him up."

Max lights up. "Best news I heard all year."

"Any one of 'em could've snatched Talulah to force Doyle to pay."

Max stops, scratches his head, thinks on it, starts pacing again. "We both know that two-bit loser couldn't ransom a postage stamp." He drives an index finger into the top of the desk. "I want the world out looking. Command post. Press. Search teams. Start from the school."

Delgado shakes his head. "Not an option. Not after your 'man-with-a-gun' stunt a few hours ago."

Max points to his watch-less wrist. "Tick Tock, Delgado. A dead granddaughter is not an option."

The lieutenant leans forward over his desk. "Maybe she just wants to be alone. She's grieving, Max."

"She's ten hashtag years old."

Delgado rolls his eyes. "Did you at least check with Doyle?"

"You know we got a history..."

"Get a hold of him. If he's no help, I'll get the word out. Also... the FBI has jurisdiction over the high seas, so I reached out to them for the cruise ship's security tapes." Delgado stands up, offers a sympathetic and worried brow. "Look, brother, if there's anything else I can do, just tell me."

"Roger that." Max nods, looks down at the leash in his hand and gives it to Delgado. "Keep an eye on the cat." With that, he rushes out the door, the lieutenant behind him expressing, rather loudly, disapproval at the exchange.

ELEVEN

DOYLE DONOVAN WALKS into Paradise Village and stops to check his mail, when his cell rings. He pulls the phone from the pocket of his old blazer, and the screen tells him it's "Dirty Harry" calling. It also tells him it's the twenty-seventh time. He ignores the call, and the ringing stops. Ten seconds later it starts again. Twenty eight.

A man in his sixties comes from around the front desk with a determined gait, his eyes on Doyle. "Doyle Donovan. You owe six months back rent."

Doyle nods toward the computer that glows from the man's station. "Not if you press delete."

"That's a felony."

"No, Oscar. That's a typo."

Oscar folds his arms across his narrow chest. "Which could put me in a six-by-nine iron cage."

"Will you take a check?" Doyle thumbs through the mail in his hand.

"I've got enough toilet paper already, thank you."

Doyle looks up from his mail. "Oscar, close your eyes a minute and picture Old Lady Scarfoli."

Oscar unfolds his arms and closes his eyes.

"You see her?"

Oscar nods.

"Now, just picture what I had to do to get this check from her."

Oscar's eyes fly open, then squint, his brow bends into a pose of anger. "That. Is. Disgusting. And don't ever do that to me again!"

"C'mon, pally. Be a mensch."

Doyle holds the check out to Oscar, then his pocket buzzes with the sound of a text alert. He checks the text from "Dirty Harry."

Stop ignoring me.

Oscar shakes his head. "Okay. Off the books or my wife's grubby paws get it. And I gotta fence the cabbage with a shylock."

"A deuce for the shylock. Three for you. Five for me. And I still owe the Village back rent."

Oscar agrees with a nod, then snatches the check from Doyle. He pulls out his billfold and counts the cash inside, when movement outside the window catches his eye. His face suddenly stretches into panic mode, eyes wide.

Outside, a yellow hummer screeches across the parking lot and steals a space away from an oncoming Lincoln Continental. The man behind the Lincoln's wheel is shriveled, hunched, and far too old to be driving. He honks, and the middle-aged driver of the hummer throws him an Italian Salute.

"It's Tommy Minetti," Oscar says. "Scram!"

Doyle snatches the check back and moves briskly down the hall. Halfway down, the door to the Community Room opens and a hand reaches out, grabs Doyle and pulls him inside.

The Paradise Village Community Room seats two-hundred patrons for various forms of entertainment: Live shows, projection-screened films, arts and crafts, and the old classic, BINGO.

Right now, it's dark, with only a sliver of light bleeding through under the door. All is quiet. Then, the scuffling of feet echo in the large room, and the lights flip on. Doyle turns toward his assailant (or savior). It's Max. With a sigh of relief, Doyle grabs his hand and shakes it. "Hey, pally! You really don't have anything to do all day, do you?"

Max squeezes back, a little too hard. He leans in—a dog with its lip curled and primed to gnash. "You seem to be in a hurry... and don't call me Pally."

Doyle lets go of his hand, turns back to the door and opens it, peeks out. Max does, too. At the front desk, Tommy Minetti—slick black hair. Thin, tall build—talks to Oscar. A gun bulges noticeably under Minetti's jacket. This guy means business.

Tommy swings his head toward them, spots Doyle and heads toward the Community Room. Max pulls him back and shuts the door, while the irate voice of the gun toter bounces down the hall. "Pay up, Doyle! You owe me twelve G's!"

"What's he want?" Max nods toward the door.

"To settle a wager." Doyle is nonplussed, waving it off.

"To settle up, huh? I smell a rat." He grips Doyle by the forearm. They're eye to eye. "Talulah is missing. Can you think of a reason why?"

Doyle cocks his head slightly. "Missing? How could she—" He drifts off, seeming to go through a list of possibilities but coming up empty. "No... I can't."

Max nods at the door again. "Has this dirtbag got the balls to snatch her?"

"Nah... Minetti's harmless."

"Then convince me otherwise. Tell me your story."

Doyle cracks a smile. "Just a little misunderstanding over a game of Texas Hold 'Em is all."

Max shakes his arm. "Listen, ya' con artist. Our granddaughter is M.I.A. Give me something to go on here."

"Maybe she went to where Cosmo worked. Did you check there?"

"No. Where's that?"

"Too hard to explain." Doyle grabs Max's arm back and pulls him toward the windows on the far side of the room. "Let's the hit the road, and I'll show you. We'll look for her together."

"Negative." Max yanks his arm away but keeps walking. "Not your getaway driver. Do not insult my intelligence."

"But Max... you make it so easy." The smile creeps back. "Seriously, we team up together and we double our chances of finding her. You *need* me."

"Like I need a heart attack. You need *me*, what with Minetti about to open that door."

"What if Talulah got snatched 'cause of you, Serpico? Ever think of that? A dirty cop you put in the big house maybe?"

They reach the far end of the room and stand by the windows, where blackout drapes cover them. Doyle pulls at one and peeks outside, as an older woman in a tracksuit jogs by.

Max looks at Doyle and shakes his head. "You allergic to nuts?"

"Why?"

"'Cause I'm gonna kick yours so far up your throat, you're gonna taste 'em."

"If I didn't know how old you are, I'd be worried."

"Worry."

Doyle sighs, reaches for the window, and pulls it open. "Well, I'm going to find Talulah." He throws a leg over.

"Maybe I've got you all wrong. Here, let me give you a hand." Max feigns helping, as he secretly slips his GPS tracker into Doyle's pocket.

Clueless about the device, Doyle hits the grass-covered ground. He stands up, brushes himself off, straightens his shirt. "Where'd you park your car, brother?"

With a sinister smile, Max shuts the window and locks it. "We ain't brothers, ya moron." He gives Doyle a wave goodbye.

Doyle shakes his head with disbelief. "For a second there, I thought I detected an actual human."

"That's why you're a moron."

Doyle points a stiff finger at the window. "Keep pushing everybody out of your life, and you're going to die all alone, ya tired, old flat foot.

Max nods toward a town car parked in the lot. The car bears the logo of The Scarfoli Family Funeral Parlor. "Looks like you're gonna die any minute, chump."

Doyle looks at the parking lot and sees the car. "Pfftt... Nicky Scarfoli's a momma's boy."

◌

Behind the wheel, inside the town car, sits a man named Fugazzi. Thirties. Cleft chin, steely eyes, and ears only a mother could love. The steelies are aimed straight at Doyle.

A man twenty years older than the driver–Mumbles Mallone–rides shotgun. His toe-plated alligator boots point north from the floorboard. He opens his mouth, and a strong stutter spills out. "W-w-why's the mortician w-w-want D-d-doyle? He's still b-b-breathing."

Fugazzi pops a piece of gum into his mouth and chews. "It's a family feud."

Doyle creeps through the parking lot, weaving in between cars to avoid the steely glare. He reaches Tommy Minetti's hummer and pulls the door handle. It gives. He dives under the steering wheel and pulls at the dash. A panel drops, and he zeros in on the wires. This isn't his first tango with hot wires. In no time, the engine is purring. He shuts the door and tucks himself behind the wheel, then backs out. The giant vehicle jerk-starts. Jerk-stops. Lurches, then slams its huge tires into a post. This *is* his first tango with a hummer.

The glass doors of Paradise Village swing open, as Tommy Minetti and his gaping maw run toward the vehicle. "Stop! Get back here! I'm gonna kill you!" Each word filled with a whiskey drinker's gruff and the rage of a hornet's nest knocked loose.

Doyle finds his footing with the Hummer and shoots past Minetti. The two make eye contact, and Doyle waves, praying Minetti's got a morsel of mercy in that oil-slicked head.

The funeral parlor town car takes chase after Doyle, while the poor, old man who'd had his parking space stolen still sits fuming in his Lincoln Continental. He slams on the pedal, races into the now-open space, and flips a bony middle finger at Minetti.

Still inside the rec room, Max snaps a picture of the town car, grits his teeth and growls. He reaches into his pocket, grabs a few Prilosec and pops them, then runs back through the room, out the door, down the hall, and to his own car.

Meanwhile, the reek of diesel fills the air as Doyle tears down the road, doing what he can to lose the Town Car, which gives chase down the four-lane road. Doyle looks in the rearview and sees Mumbles open the sunroof. The stuttering man pokes out the top of the car holding a gun. He takes aim, then fires at the Hummer. At Doyle.

Bullets whiz around the yellow tank, and Doyle's palms go slick with sweat, knuckles white across the wheel. He's not handling the gas hog well at all, as though the steering has a mind of its own, swerving left, right. Right, left.

Horns honk, tires screech and skid, as the surrounding traffic takes heed. A few cars collide, not so lucky in this spontaneous freeway obstacle course.

Behind Doyle, a window sprays glass across the backseat, followed by quick pinging thuds, as the bullets search him out.

Mumbles continues taking shots, standing through the open sunroof. Doyle and the Hummer zig zag, narrowly missing oncoming cars, as the bullets fly. Suddenly, it takes a sharp left, rips through traffic cones, ignores the signs on either side of the road that read CONSTRUCTION SITE AHEAD. Dust flies in the vehicle's wake.

A bullet takes out the sideview mirror on the driver's side, and Doyle ducks under the dash, watching the camera monitor to steer. In the chaos, his arm bumps a button on the dash, activating the Voice Control Feature, and a female voice starts to speak.

"Hello. This is your friendly Skypal Assistance Concierge. How is your day going so far, Mr. Minetti?"

The voice startles Doyle. He sits up and cranes his neck, looks around. A bullet takes out the rearview, and he ducks again, steering the best he can through the monitor, struggling to keep the vehicle on the road. "Hello? Can you hear me?" he asks the woman's voice.

"Yes, sir. What excellent service may I provide you with today?"

"I'd like to order a pizza."

Doyle blasts into a construction site, passing a crane,

narrowly missing a cement truck. A worker nearby drops his jaw, as he feeds it a pastrami sub.

The town car follows, with Mumbles standing up through the open hatch like an armed figurehead. He ducks to the left, just missing the crane, then back to firing, as the driver leaves his own trail of dust.

Doyle clips a dumpster with the Humvee, then rockets into the path of a fuel truck. Crunched down further under the dash like a scared child, he slams on the gas pedal with one hand, while the other keeps its trembling grip on the wheel. He keeps his eyes glued to the monitor, waiting for the inevitable explosion, then does his best to swerve from a fiery death.

The fuel truck puts forth its own effort and brakes, turns hard and skids broadside, just missing the oncoming Hummer. An Andy Gump port-a-potty takes the hit instead, sending the bright-blue thing airborne. Mumbles watches the soaring toilet somersault end over end, heading straight for him, and ducks for cover inside the town car.

The port-a-potty crashes on top of the car, flooding a weeks' worth of human waste from sweaty city workers in through the sunroof.

Despite the valiant attempt, Doyle slams into the fuel truck, then the town car joins the collision chaos by rear-ending Doyle. Teeth rattle and necks whiplash, as flames begin to tickle the underside of the town car. The tinkering noise of engines settling fill the silence in the aftermath, while fuel leaks from under the Hummer. A moment later, Murphy's Law pulls the fuel toward the flames.

Doyle gets out of the vehicle, stretches, twists, and cracks his back. Mere feet away, gas creeps toward the explosive catalyst.

☖

Max squints at the phone mounted on the dash of his Cressida, watching the small, blinking dot on the screen of the GPS app as it moves, representing the tiny unit inside Doyle's pocket. Too easy. He cracks a smile as he cruises along.

○

Doyle surveys the damage. The back end of the Hummer seems to have fended off the town car hit impressively well. The front end, however, has seen better days. A broken axle tilts the left front tire inward, while the hood is crumpled like tinfoil.

An orange flicker catches his eye, subtle enough to almost miss. But the hue is familiar, and the imminent danger registers immediately. The town car is on fire. Tiny flames lick the underside of it, as the glow brightens.

Doyle races toward the fuel truck, throws open the driver's side door and finds the driver unconscious. He wrestles with the seatbelt and pulls the driver out, dragging him several yards down the street, crossing it, then into a patch of overgrown grass, far enough away from any impending explosion.

On shaky legs, Doyle staggers back into the street, and a small car with a light-box on its roof reading LIGHTNING PIZZA slows to a stop beside him. The side of the car declares *15-Minute Delivery or it's FREE!* The vehicle stops, and a college-aged middle-eastern driver rolls down the passenger window. There's concern across his face as he scans the scene of the accident. "Mr. Minetti?" he says to Doyle, then pulls a pizza box from a warming bag and tries to hand it through the window.

Instead, Doyle opens the car door, slides in, takes the

60

box, flips the lid, and grabs a slice. The driver's mouth is stuck open, a question or two on his tongue.

Doyle breaks the silence. "Well, those two shitheads ain't Minetti, pally." He points down the street, where Fugazzi and Mumbles crawl from the town car, covered in brown. "What took so long?" He takes another bite of pizza.

Fugazzi wipes frantically at his face, trying to clear it of excrement, while his buddy runs away gagging, falls to his knees down the road, and starts heaving into the grass.

"I'd step on it or they're going to think you're a terrorist," Doyle says, nestled in the passenger seat, a mouthful of extra cheese.

Pizza Guy tilts his head in confusion. "But I'm not a terrorist."

"You don't have to convince *me*."

He barely gets the words out before the town car explodes, then the Hummer, followed by the fuel truck. The blasts shake the small car, and Pizza Guy floors it. He does a quick one-eighty, and leaves the two lackeys in the rearview, as they recover on the side of the road.

TWELVE

THE PIZZA CAR pulls up outside a skate shop. An attached skatepark stretches across the property. A fence surrounds the acreage, while within its bounds skateboarders are hard at practice. Bowls, handrails, half pipes, quarter pipes, launch ramps, a snake run, and boxes. It's all here.

Max parks behind the shop and turns off the tracking app. He gets out of the car. A few kids line the coping of a vert ramp on the other side of a fence. One drops in, carves, then launches off the coping at least ten feet, does a few twists, grabs his tail, and lands. His buddies cheer.

Doyle gets out of the delivery driver's car with a slice in his hand. He spots Max. "How'd you find this place, pally?" He offers the slice to Max, who is approaching with a determined stride.

Max ignores the pizza and reaches quickly into Doyle's pocket, fetching the GPS tracking unit. "Quit calling me that, ya piker. Where's the yellow tank?"

"Ran out of gas. Darn thing gets terrible mileage." The pizza smacks in Doyle's mouth when he talks. "Spot me a twenty? I left my wallet in the Hummer."

The pizza driver looks at Max like a puppy waiting to be fed. Max grumbles, reaches for his wallet, and pays the man for the food.

Doyle hands the box, and the rest of the pizza in it, to a bicycle rental vendor next to the skate shop. "Here. Take it. My partner's got reverse hypoglycemia."

Max's eyes turn to slits. "We're not partners!"

Doyle smirks and heads for the skate shop. Inside, the walls are lined with skateboard decks and T-shirts. There's a few large racks displaying the latest in BMX bikes. Rows of hardware, swag, and other skateboard-adjacent items, like Razors and scooters.

Doyle grabs a complete deck and tests his weight on it. He pushes off and zips down an aisle filled with trucks, wheels, wax, and grip-tape. He spins, stops in front of the store manager—a woman in her twenties who fills out a pair of spandex in a way that has Doyle's eyes linger for too long.

"A sexagenarian on a skateboard. I'm impressed," she says, hands on her hips.

Doyle grins. "Emphasis on the sex. Doyle Donovan at your service. Miss...?"

"Ursula." She smiles back, but it's not flirty. More like charity, something she'd offer the crazy uncle at Thanksgiving. "Can I help you?"

"Ahh, yes. Ursula. The Great Bear goddess in command of the constellation Ursa Major and ruler of eleven thousand virgins." His eyes trail the spandex. "Indeed a goddess. Do you give lessons?"

"Goddess or skateboard?"

The bell above the shop door rings as Max enters. Doyle points a thumb toward him. "Susan's old man. Emphasis on the old."

Max storms through the rows of merch and catches up with them. "Do you know Cosmo Donovan?"

"My *son*." Doyle offers. It's a prideful declaration, with a hint of somber.

A weight suddenly pulls at Ursula's face. "I'm so sorry for your loss. Cosmo was amazing. A true prodigy."

"Back to business," Max says, "Did he have any money problems?"

Ursula retracts like she's dodging a bumblebee. "That's none of your business."

A door creaking open in the back grabs Max's attention. He squints, tilts his head left and right. "What's going on back there?"

Behind the door are three young men in a workshop. A few workbenches littered with tools and hardware line the far wall. Two desks, each with their own computer sit in the center. The largest of the men—at least three-hundred pounds—stands at the door, eavesdropping.

"That's also none of your business." He can hear Ursula say, followed by a rebuttal from Max. "Cosmo lived with my daughter, Doll Face. I need some information here."

"Check this out," the heavy man signals to his coworkers. "Two more guys here asking about Cosmo."

Max sees movement through the crack in the door and spots the giant eavesdropper. "Hey! Back there!" Makes a run for the door. "I've got questions for you!" He slams into the door and crashes into big Wally. Hard. Max bounces back like he hit a wall.

One of the other guys, whose hat sits backward, short, tiny dreads poking out from under like pointy bleached bones, yells out, "Leerooooy Jenkinnsss!!!" He and his skinny Asian buddy, with a ponytail and ratty camouflage shorts peppered with hand sewn patches, hop on their boards, weave through the desks and head for the backdoor. Wally follows behind on his own board, the weight of him giving the seven-ply deck an unhealthy flex. All three twenty-somethings reach the back door, push through, and bolt outside.

Max limp-runs after. "Stay right where you are!"

The back door leads straight into the skatepark. Max reaches the door and looks out. He sees the three guys on the half pipe. Two drop in, Wally—already winded—looks back, sees Max. He drops in. All three transition to another ramp, then a bowl, where they launch up and over the fence.

Max runs after, prepared to climb the fence but finds a gap in it first and races through. "Get back here!"

Doyle appears from out of nowhere, sitting on a bright red rental bike built for two. "Hop on."

Against his better judgment, Max swings a rusty leg over and hops on. "You better know what you're doing."

"Absolutely," Doyle says. "No problem."

The two pedal forward, and the bike takes off down the street, picking up speed toward a convoy of cars. Swerving, dodging, and a handful of near misses, gets them turned around, which Max points out through a panicky declaration. "You're going the wrong way!"

"Not a problem." Doyle makes a quick U-turn. Max nearly loses his balance, and his knuckles go white as the two find themselves in the path of an Arrowhead Water truck.

Max shouts, "Truck!"

"*That's* a problem!"

The water truck takes a sharp, quick right, bounces onto a curb, and mows down a row of newspaper machines that drop like cardboard boxes, all in a line. Finally, a large oak tree stops the wayward journey. Bottles of water explode from the truck and fly through the air. It rains.

Doyle and Max zig-zag across the busy street, and Max lifts his legs, unable to keep up with the speed of the pedals, his knee popping. "We're losing them!" he yells. "Go faster! Go! Go!"

"You got pedals, too! Pump!"

Max doesn't want to admit his aching leg isn't up to the task, admit that maybe he's too old to be chasing young adults on skateboards, even if one of them is fat and lagging hopelessly behind the others.

An oncoming SUV seems to pop out of nowhere, and Doyle turns last minute. The sudden turn takes them into the path of a canary-yellow Volkswagen Bug impossible to miss, yet Doyle makes another successful swerve, and they narrowly avoid collision.

Ahead, two of the boarders ollie over a steel barricade, landing in a newly paved parking lot where a farmer's market has set up shop. Big Wally thinks better of the attempt and picks up his board, walks around the barricade, then sets the board down, and the wood creaks again as he puts it to the test with all three-hundred pounds.

Doyle barrels around a corner, and the sight of a crossing guard holding up a sign makes his mouth go dry.

"Move!" Max screams at the children crossing. "Get outta the way!" He screams at the guard.

Doyle tilts and swerves, barely clipping the guard's sleeve. The front tire of the bike nicks the end of a barricade, and the metal thing swings outward. The bike's handlebars brush against a produce stand, and Max's leg hits a crate of lemons, spilling them to the ground like tennis balls.

The skaters up ahead, dodge and weave much more successfully than the two older men. Even Wally manages to conjure some grace.

Max's eyes go wide at a sight up ahead. "Doyle! Watch out for the baby!"

"Baby?"

Max wants to point, but he doesn't dare let go. Instead, he tightens his grip and offers a silent prayer.

"I don't see a—" Doyle quickly pulls a pair of glasses from his front pocket and puts them on with just enough time to see the carriage. He cuts around it but smashes through a popcorn stand. It snows, butter flavored.

The skaters make a right and find themselves in an alley filled with dumpsters. A locked metal gate blocks any exit. Dead end. Wheels screech and tails hit pavement, as they turn around and head back towards Max & Doyle, racing past the oncoming bike built for two.

"Turn around! Turn. Turn!!" Max yells.

"Hey," Doyle counters. "Nobody likes a backseat driver." But Doyle honors the panicked request and turns. Chaos ensues, and people jump out of the way. A woman clutches her purse and dives into the arms of a stranger paying for a bouquet of flowers, while a man and his son jump away from the oncoming bike, knocking into the flower stand. Petals explode, littering the ground.

"Sorry!" Doyle yells, as the bike whips past the pedestrians.

Somewhere ahead, the skaters cut down another alley.

"You lost 'em." Max huffs, his legs tired from holding them up.

Doyle darts ahead and jumps a curb. The bike bounces, jarring them both, and Max's teeth clack together. Unable to swerve in time, they crash into a dress vendor. Doyle ducks his head, and a dress envelopes his passenger. When they rip around the corner, Max is cocooned within a sequined dress.

"No I haven't. Look!" Doyle says, nodding up ahead.

Max peels the dress from his face and looks. There they are, all back at the skatepark. Stalled, with seemingly nowhere else to go. "There's no way out," Max says. "We've got 'em! Turn on the steam."

"A little help back there?"

Max puts his feet on the pedals and pushes, putting every bit of effort into it, determined to keep up with Doyle's pace, despite the bad knee. He stands with each push, head down, gritting his teeth through the grind of his knee. When he looks up again, the skaters are gone. "Where'd they go?"

The older men keep their pace, failing to see they've reached the top of a halfpipe flush with the pavement. It's too late to stop. They drop into the ten-foot vertical ramp. Stomachs turn, grips tighten, and butts clench.

"Aaaaaahhhhhh!" The cacophonic rasp of aging men fills the park, while onlookers add to the choir with cheering.

One kid raises a fist, "Right on!"

Another doubles over in laughter. "Go, geezers, go!"

As the men descend the ramp, they pick up speed and race up the vertical climb. Each man shifts his weight forward, not out of a great understanding of physics in a life-or-death moment but out of pure terror, as they white knuckle the handlebars. The shift in weight launches them into the air, up and over the coping and the platform, where astounded kids have cleared a path. But it's the landing that feels like divine intervention more than good old-fashioned luck, as the two-seated biked drops on top of the dazed group of skaters they'd been chasing.

Max peels his eyes open, looks around. Sees the Scooby-Doo style capture, and holds back a grin behind a pain in his side, where the handlebar has met it. He looks at the pile of kids under him. "Why were you all running?"

Wally rubs his head where a pedal had caught him. "Because you were chasing us."

Max points a shaking finger. "You need to tell us what you can, son. My granddaughter is missing, and I'll do whatever it takes to find her. I'd give my life for that little girl."

The big boy cocks a bleeding eyebrow. "Man... that is stupid."

"Not really. Talulah is the only person in my life who ever loved me unconditionally, and—"

Doyle puts a hand on Max's shoulder, closes his eyes, gives his head a sympathetic shake.

Finally, Wally caves. "A couple Asian dudes came by last week asking questions about Cosmo. That's all I know."

The kid with the bleached dreads, his hat no longer hiding the natty mess. "One had a scar across his face. The other one was jurassic, with Chinese tats all over his scalp."

"Why would Chinese tough guys be interested in Cosmo?" Max asks.

The skinny guy with the pony tail picks at a fresh rip in his shorts. "Cosmo was a partner in our start-up company, Sugar Plum. He was amazing, man. Our secret sauce, ya know?"

While the skaters get up and pull themselves together, Max ponders what Cosmo could have done to get in so much trouble with a group of Chinese thugs. Worse yet, how'd he manage to drag Susan into it?

○

Inside the skate shop's office, Doyle, Max, Ursula, and the skaters huddle around a computer monitor. On the screen, a digital design of a skateboard with dime-sized, high-tech computer chips on each wheel.

With the mouse in Wally's hand, he spins the 3-D image. "There's never been a skateboard like this, Gramps.

Cosmo's design will revolutionize skateboard competition. Worldwide."

Drop-shot—Asian, ponytail—points to one of the wheels, "A micro computer monitors weight, balance, and speed."

Nose-pick—ballcap with the dreads. "Then it processes the information and adjusts the requisite tension on each wheel."

Ursula looks at Max, pride across her face. "Drop-shot got his M.A. from Berkley. Wally has a PhD from Cornell. Nose-pick got his double "E" from M.I.T. I studied design at F.I.T. And Susan was working to take our start-up company public."

Wally swings his head around, looks up at Doyle. "The patent will be worth billions."

"We finished the prototype," says Nose-pick.

Drop-shot lowers his head in mourning, shakes it. "And now it's missing."

Max studies the skateboard on the screen, an image that to him has always been nothing more than a toy. But now it's a missing prototype worth billions. Things are starting to make sense.

THIRTEEN

Kowloon Harbor, Hong Kong

LASER LIGHTS DANCE across the city, attracted like moths to flame on one building in particular–Chimera Corporation, a looming monolith with its oppressively giant emblem in full view of the pedestrian-ants below.

Inside the office penthouse, a nervous servant pours tea for Mr. Chan–a Chinese billionaire in his forties, who is busy pinning a butterfly into a velvet-lined case, the insect's wings fluttering wildly as it desperately tries to escape.

An intrusive sound comes through the nearby speakers of a computer, and the oversized monitor blinks the announcement of an incoming video call. Mr. Chan reaches over and taps the screen, accepting the call. The scarred face of a middle-aged Chinese man appears. Chan sips his tea, then sets the cup down before addressing him. "Greetings, Wang Tzu."

Chan's servant stands nearby, trembling in fear, causing the kettle to clink against the cup as he pours a refill.

"Thank you for your audience, Mr. Chan," Wang Tzu says.

The butterfly's spine makes an audible pop as the pin breaks through, adhering the beautiful thing to its velvet coffin forever.

Chan keeps his eyes on his powder-wing trophy. "I trust you have good news. I am not accustomed to disappointment."

"The mission was a success, and the transfer is scheduled for tomorrow night. I think now is the time we renegotiate the terms of my duty."

There's a smugness across Wang Tzu's face. Pride. The tattooed head of Xhing enters the screen, his muscled arms bulging under a shirt that fits like a second skin. The behemoth wears a grin of his own.

Mr. Chan's hands fumble with the velvety display case as he closes the glass lid with his thumb. "Renegotiate?"

"I want an equal share," Wang Tzu pauses, waits for a response.

Chan's thumb presses hard on the box lid, and the glass spiderwebs, splitting his skin.

"They both had refused to sign," Wang Tzu says, tilting his head as he listens to the grinding of glass against flesh. "Neither of them care if they live or die. We need both signatures."

Wang moves to the side, giving Xhing the room he and his muscles need to show he now holds Talulah. The big man's grin widens, carrying with it evil intent.

"I'll be there tomorrow," Chan says. "As planned." He taps the screen to end the call, and a drop of blood runs down it.

FOURTEEN

OUTSIDE THE SURF and skate shop in Venice Beach, Doyle follows Max, matching his every step, maybe a little too closely. But there's urgency here.

"We need intelligence," Doyle says.

"Whaddya mean 'we'? You got a midget in your pocket?" Max walks faster, an effort to put some space between the two.

"I know one very resourceful cat."

"I'll work my own snitches. Old Ray Jay Perkins. He'll talk to me." Ray Jay was known around the community for having an ear to the ground, particularly in the sections where trouble seemed to find you. No map needed. But in this case Ray Jay was easy to find because he was usually already in the middle of trouble. Small-time stuff, almost to the point of being harmless, but he rubbed elbows with the bigger sharks.

"Yeah. Well, you'll be the only one he's talking to," Doyle says. "'Cause Old Ray Jay's got Alzheimer's."

Max stops. "I'm so sorry. I had no idea." Picks back up. "Wait... I know. I got a long-time acquaintance– Soul Patch. But I'll need his twenty."

"Try Sing-Sing, dum-dum."

Max scratches his head. "Okay... well, you mentioned an acquaintance?"

"Yeah. Whatever goes down, my guy hears about it. Some yo-yo spits on the sidewalk, and he's got his name, address, blood type, and shoe size."

Max reaches the Cressida. "So, who is this omniscient wonder?"

"Ernie Malloy. Big ears." Doyle holds his hands out from the side of his head, as though displaying Dumbo-sized ears. "He's my bookie."

"Where can I find him?"

"He's shacked up with Lola, the fortune teller. C'mon Dick Tracy... let's go pay our respects." Doyle tries for the passenger door. "Door's locked."

"Good. I do it to keep criminals, like you, out." Max opens the driver's side door.

Doyle races around to Max's side. "Teaming up with you, I had no expectations, and so far, you haven't let me down." He tries to push past Max and squeeze into the driver's seat, but Max grabs him by the lapels and pulls him back.

"I'd rather try to get smoke inside a bottle using a baseball bat than team up with a lowlife like you." Max's eyes are locked onto Doyle's, sending the message loud and clear.

Doyle isn't having it and grabs back, each in the other's grip. Some tugging, some scuffling. "Easy there, Lone Ranger. This is a three-thousand-dollar suit!"

Max pushes off the car and into Doyle, knocking him back. "Somebody call nine-one-one. This bum's gonna need an ambulance!"

Within seconds, the two grown men manage to have each other in variations of a headlock, while an inquisitive crowd gathers. Someone cheers, and the vocal contagion spreads to the rest of the crowd. Two waiters from the patio of a nearby Vietnamese café place bets.

"I got fifty bucks on the geezer in the suit."

"Put me down for twenty."

The headlocks are loosed, and Max throws a haymaker. Doyle ducks.

"My ninety-five-year-old Aunt Betty throws a better punch than you, and she just had a stroke," Doyle taunts.

Max cocks back for a right cross, and Doyle looks for help, his eyes searching the crowd and beyond. Before delivery of the punch, a police officer swoops in and catches Max's arm, pulls him back. "Whoa! Hold up there, old timer."

"Old timer?" Max growls "I still got lead in my pencil!"

Doyle nods, backs away. "I gotta go see my Aunt Betty and check on her stroke." He disappears into the crowd as it disperses.

Max yanks his arm away. "I'm your brother officer."

"You mean *'retired'* brother officer." The policeman's tag reads Mulgrew. He helps brush dusty pavement off Max's jacket.

Max gasps for breath and lets out a sigh. He pushes Mulgrew's hands away. "You know who I am?"

"Roger that." The officer hooks thumbs in his belt. "At the academy, our instructors told us all about the time you didn't want to wait for back-up."

Max shakes his head, tired of hearing the same 'ole. "And I still don't." He shoves past the cop. "Out of my way, Rookie." And starts into the car. "You're wasting my time."

Max climbs in, starts up, and takes off. For the next few miles, his mind is on that day he didn't wait for backup. While he's sour about the outcome in regard to how his career was plucked from him, he doesn't regret the decision he made to head into battle. He sticks by every call made that day, and when he meets his maker on judgment day, it'll be with confidence and the knowledge of a job well done.

FIFTEEN

MAX PULLS his Cressida to a stop at the curb outside a nail salon. The lights from the city drown out the stars in an otherwise filled sky as people walk the street. An Italian ice vendor pushes a cart with a squeaky wheel. A group of young woman in tight skirts awkwardly balance their drunken selves on shiny heels, narrowly avoiding cracks in the sidewalk. Above the salon, a second-floor entrance sign reads: *Madame Lola Reads Past, Present, and Future – Lotto Tickets Sold Here!*

Max opens the glovebox, pulls out his gun. Old faithful. It's always there when ready. He gets out of the car and heads up to the second story, toward the sign and the door under it. He pushes the doorbell. It rings out to the tune of *Whatever Lola Wants*. He doesn't wait long before an elderly woman opens the door. The skin from her arms hangs like parchment. Her hunched posture is covered in layers of purple, and large, golden hoops pull at her melting earlobes.

Max reaches for his badge. "I'm—"

Before he can finish the introduction, Madame Lola

dramatically puts a palm to her forehead. "...Detective Maximillian Tyrell."

"I need–"

She swings an arm, gesturing him in. A collection of bracelets jangle across her forearm. "...to see Big Ears."

Max enters, looks around. The room has a dark pink hue to it, as though under the glow of a motel sign. A crystal ball illuminates on a small table in the corner of the room. The table sports a long, draping cloth full of moons and stars. Faint, solemn accordion music is heard coming through a glass-bead curtain that divides this room from whatever's beyond.

Lola points toward the curtain, her finger gnarled and held captive by a giant, gaudy ring. "Your friend Doyle's in there."

Max snarls a lip at the word *"friend."* "We ain't friends."

Lola stares back, incredulously, "Keep telling yourself that," as Max walks through the curtain. It clinks softly as it yields to him. From somewhere in the crowded room, a parrot squawks. Other than candelabras and an impressive amount of flower arrangements, there are people. Unsavory characters. Street people. A man with an accordion, wearing neighborhood ads across his back and a parrot on his shoulder, plays his instrument at a quiet volume. The parrot on his shoulder whistles at an attractive Puerto Rican woman dressed in tight, revealing clothes, giving the impression her work is done behind a bedroom door. She walks to Doyle, who sits in an overstuffed chair in the corner.

"Rosie," Doyle says. "You never age."

When Rosie speaks, her voice is deep, manly. "Hey, Doyle. Want a blow job? On the house?"

"What's in it for me?"

Max walks over to them. "I'm here to talk to old Big Ears."

The parrot interjects. "Squawk. Big ears! Big ears! Squawk!"

"He may be a little hard of hearing these days." Rosie points across the room, where at first glance Max thinks a sofa sits, but on closer look, it's a casket. Inside, Big Ears is dressed like a jockey, his coffin resting on a funeral bier with wheels. "Big Ears passed on to that great big horse track in the sky. He was truly revered by our community."

"Saved my ass a couple times, I'll tell ya," Doyle adds. "You needed info, you'd call Big Ears. Not four-one-one. A real clutch hitter. Helluva handicapper, too. Great on long shots."

"Lost big-time on Johnson's Johnson yesterday in the third at Belmont," Rosie says.

"Uh, oh," Doyle says. "That is not good news."

Max takes a few steps and looks down at the coffin, studies the body inside. "How'd he buy it?"

Rosie says, "Last night, Lola gives him a bowl of her homemade minestrone soup. He tells her it's the best soup he's ever tasted. Then he farts, says 'pardon me', and keels over. Dead. Face first into the minestrone."

"I've had Lola's minestrone," Doyle shares a personal moment. "It's absolutely fabulous."

Max makes a mental note to never try it.

◌

A couple of tough guys pass through the beaded curtain and enter the funeral: Two Fingers—aptly named—and Hawk Eye, who wears an eye patch. Hawk Eye lays his one good eye on Doyle. "Is that Doyle Donovan?"

"In the flesh," Two Fingers says. "So what?"

"Could be our pipeline to Fort Knox." Hawk Eye stuffs

a finger under his patch and buries it deep, scratching an itch in the void.

"Doyle ain't got two dimes to rub together to make a quarter."

Rosie spots the two, the expressions on their faces, the look in their eyes. With concern, she points them out. "Doyle. Over there. Eyes on you. Closer than my five o'clock shadow." The tough guys look away, acting oblivious and uninterested. Rosie changes the subject but stays alert. "Got plans for tonight? Me and my posse are putting on a show at your old folks house. Want a free comp?"

"Sorry, Rosie. My granddaughter's missing. We were hoping Big Ears heard something."

Rosie looks at Doyle. "That's just... just terrible."

Max speaks up. "Know anything about two Chinese gangsters? One with a scar across his face, and a tree trunk with tats on his scalp? Seen 'em around?"

"Yeah," Rosie says. "I heard about two guys like that running working girls out of some dry cleaner up in China Town."

Across the room, Hawk Eye pulls out a phone and makes a call. "Doyle upset The Mortician."

"And you do not want to upset The Mortician," Two Fingers says. "He embalms people."

"While they are still alive sometimes." Hawk Eye raises the phone slightly. "He'll show us his appreciation for this call." Then pushes it close to his ear, speaks into it. "Mr. Scarfoli? It's Hawk Eye."

♡

Across town, at the Scarfoli Family Funeral Home, a hearse pulls out of the garage.

SIXTEEN

A GROUP of selected pallbearers wheel the bier holding Big Ears' coffin down the hall toward the stairwell. Mourners follow, some whispering prayers, some quietly singing, others whimpering and wiping away the tears. They descend the stairs, and a crowd gathers at the bottom. And there's Tommy Minetti. He stands on the street curb, slowly pulling a gun from inside his blazer.

Hawk Eye sees the gun. "Be prepared to duck," he says.

Two Fingers looks at him, his brow twisted with confusion. "Duck? For what?"

From the curb, Minetti raises the gun, levels it. "Doyle Donovan! I'm gonna kill you!"

He fires.

Two Fingers and his one-eyed buddy duck down. "Now I get it."

Minetti keeps his finger on the trigger, and bullets fly, sinking into plaster and splitting wood. Max and Doyle do their best to dodge, unsure if it'll do any good but throw the dice anyway.

"Minetti's harmless, huh?" Max pushes Rosie and her

friends down, for cover. "Stay down!" The group huddles behind pillars on the second floor.

"Hey, Rambo. You gonna do something?" Doyle asks.

Max takes out his phone, dials. A single ring and Delgado picks up on the other end. "That call for backup...?" Max yells over the gunfire. "Here it is, so you'd better step on it."

Bullets burrow with a vengeance into the pillars, as well as the walls behind them. The air fills with clouds of sawdust and drywall.

"You were a problem on the job, and you're still one today, Retired!" Delgado huffs.

"Listen! Some two-bit crook is trying to pump lead into Doyle."

"Alright. Rolling backup now," Delgado says. "And, Max? This time, wait for it."

The call ends, and Minetti fires another bullet.

"Use your gun!" Doyle says.

"Delgado said to wait for backup."

"We'll be dead by then. Shoot!" A splinter of wood lands in Doyle's hair.

Max shakes his head. "Nope. Made that mistake once."

A bullet screams by Doyle's head, and he jumps to his feet. In a spontaneously desperate move, he shoves the funeral bier toward the stairs. The coffin slides forward, somersaults end over end down the stairs. Big Ears launches from the casket, flies through the air, and crashes into the Italian ice vendor.

"Well, that didn't go as planned." Doyle looks to the ducking mourners. "Perchance, are any of you poor, dear, bereaving souls packing heat?"

More than one responds by pulling their guns from holsters, blazers, ankles, and belts. The funeral goers return fire on Minetti, and he makes a hasty retreat, running off between cars. Doyle and Max head down the stairs.

"How many goons you got after you?" Max asks.

"I don't know. Maybe six? Seven? I'm into some loan sharks, and then there's my gambling markers. Could be eight or nine."

Bullets fly from the mourner's guns, and Minetti continues his retreat toward the fisherman's wharf, while Doyle and Max make a break for the Cressida. Out of breath, they crouch down and perch behind it, using the car for cover. Doyle says, "That's Tommy Minetti shooting at us. Can you hit him from here?"

Max points to the right side of his head. "You gotta talk in my right ear, my left side's bad."

Doyle huffs, then shouts into Max's right ear. "Can you hit him from here?!"

"Can I hit him from here?! I can't even see him from here!"

"Try these on, Mr. Magoo." Doyle takes out his glasses, puts them on Max.

Minetti reaches his own car and climbs in, then aims and sends an onslaught of bullets, which pepper Max's car. His beautiful Cressida. That does it! Max draws his gun, peeks above the Cressida's hood, and fires. The side mirror of Minetti's car shatters and hangs like a dead limb. Another bullet spiderwebs Max's windshield. Max returns fire with three more shots, while Minetti drives off.

Max stands, and his knee pops. "Jiminy Cricket!" He dusts himself off, takes the glasses off his face and hands them back to Doyle.

"Keep 'em."

"Know what I like about you?" Max asks.

"No. What?"

"Nothin'!"

They get in the car. Gaping holes in the windshield but enough to see through, enough to catch a bug in the eye once they hit the road. There's a few new holes in the seats, one of them being in the driver's side headrest. Doyle swallows hard as he surveys the damage. "Damn shame about your car. So, what now, pally?"

Max shoves the barrel of his gun under Doyle's chin. "Listen up, *pally*! You got a price on your head, and I don't have a death wish. I'll find Talulah on my own. Now, get out and stay away from me!"

Doyle pays no mind to the threat and spots the gleaming badges of two uniformed policemen through his side of the car. He points them out to Max. "Okay, Bronson, our backup is here. But I got three-to-one says I find her before you!" He exits the car with a quickness and slams the door. Max starts the car, throws it into gear, and burns rubber.

Outside the car, Doyle gets a better look at the "cops." It's not backup after all but impostors. Fugazzi and Mumbles, like a couple of piranha, stalking a pair of wading shins. Fugazzi giggles at him, then goes in for a bite.

In an effort to blow their cover, Doyle quickly points at Mumbles' toe-plated alligator boots, hoping Max catches the signal in his rear view.

He does.

He watches as they force Doyle into a Scarfoli hearse, a gun pointed at Doyle's side. Max shakes his head and slams his fist on the steering wheel, over and over. "I'm getting too old for this shit!"

The hearse speeds away, and Max makes a U-turn, sideswiping two cars, then jumping the curb. He takes out a parking kiosk, and the thing pops open. Coins litter the street. People nearby scream, holler, and dive for cover.

Max curses the shattered windshield and fixes his eyes on the back of the hearse, wondering what kind of wisecracks the idiot's giving these guys, even with a gun in his side. "You've made your bed, Doyle Donovan. I oughta just let you sleep in it."

Max floors the pedal, and the Cressida purrs.

SEVENTEEN

INSIDE THE SCARFOLI'S Family Funeral Home.

Funeral director Lydia Scarfoli leads a group of mourners through a brief introduction of the family business, a smile on her face as fake as her hip. Max has blended in with the crowd, doing his best to look inconspicuous. He scans the room while the woman speaks.

"Scarfoli's Family Funeral Home is a high-tech mortuary, providing services for every religion." The woman holds a remote in her hand, occasionally giving a showcasing twist of her wrist while she talks. "We strive to make sure each and every–" She finds herself distracted as Max takes off his jacket, wraps it around his gun. This doesn't go unnoticed, and her finger searches for the little red button on the remote. She pushes it.

In the basement of the building, inside the embalming room, Mumbles hands Fugazzi his police uniform, and a warning light on the wall flashes red. Fugazzi takes the uniform, puts it on a hangar, hangs it on a rack next to his own SFPD disguise. Mumbles spots the red flashing light, draws his gun, and heads out of the lab to deal with the alert. Fugazzi stays behind, along with Nick Scarfoli, who turns to face the man standing against the far wall. It's Doyle Donovan. He is not happy.

Doyle forces the grin of a Cheshire Cat, "Hi'ya pally, heard you were looking for me."

Nick returns a smile of his own. "Doyle Donovan. You worthless, philandering, gold-digging, charlatan!"

"You make that sound like it's a bad thing."

Scarfoli's smile is calm and gentle, the kind that holds back an onslaught, one that could be loosed at any moment. He pats the embalming table in the middle of the room, keeping the smile intact. "Have a seat right here."

Doyle's skin goes prickly. Sweat instantly bleeds from his pores. Fight or flight. He chooses fight and jams a quick elbow into Fugazzi's gut. Hard! Fugazzi drops his gun and makes a desperate attempt to grab for Doyle, but the older man is quick from the panic and swings an IV stand like a baseball bat. Fugazzi dodges it, and the stand hits the wall, exploding the bag attached. The two grapple, wrestling for the upper hand, until Scarfoli steps in, firmly grabs Doyle, and injects him with a needle. Doyle crumbles, lifeless and snoring.

◯

Back in the funeral home parlor, Lydia stands at the podium, remote in her hand. "Our bereaved have given us photos and videos of their dearly departed, which we have incorporated into a memorial tribute." She offers a sympathetic smile over the small, seated crowd. "Let us begin." She presses a button, and the curtains part, the lights dim, and a video on a large screen begins.

In the back of the room, Max pays no mind to the slideshow and instead keeps his eyes on the crowd,

87

watching for any sudden movement from the darkened corners of the parlor.

But Mumbles finds him first, and the barrel of a gun pushes against his spine. Max snarls, and a hand reaches inside his jacket, takes his gun.

⬠

Doyle stirs awake, his lids still heavy from whatever he'd been sedated with. He goes to sit up and finds he can't move. A quick glance down shows his arms strapped to his side by leather restraints. The sudden awareness of an aching back tells him he's on a hard surface–Yes, of course– the embalming table he'd been invited to sit on. Looking up reveals the IV stand upright again. The bag has been replaced, and the drip tube stops at his arm, while the needle end is buried under a wide band of medical tape, covering the hole in his skin. Despite the glaring evidence around him, he does his best to ignore the idea he's about to be embalmed. Alive.

"I had a dream like this once," he says through a smile that struggles to hide the concern. "It didn't end well."

Nick Scarfoli appears over him, a rubber apron covering plum-hued Armani. He wipes his hands on the apron. "The restraints are for your own protection... when you're thrashing."

"Thrashing!?"

The corners of Scarfoli's mouth turn upward gleefully. "From the pain." He giggles.

"You must really hate me." Doyle tests the strength of the restraints. Sturdy as can be. He's not going anywhere.

Fugazzi steps in, makes sure Doyle can see his face. "Maybe bangin' Mr. Scarfoli's momma was not such a good idea."

Scarfoli holds a hand out. "Our cocktail, please, Mr. Fugazzi."

Fugazzi reaches for the large syringe lying on a tray next to the embalming table. He hands it over, and Scarfoli injects the contents into the hanging IV bag.

"There's gotta be some way I can..." Doyle watches the button on the IV drip, waiting for one of them to push it. "...something I can—"

"Relax. Nothing happens 'til I push the button." Scarfoli nods toward the object of Doyle's attraction. "Then that machine there..." The man points to a device that looks like a four-gallon blender with a hose protruding from it. "...that'll pump poison right through your body, causing excruciating pain. And a very, slow death, of course."

Doyle's eyes widen in terror, and thrash is exactly what he does. Pure desperation. His voice cracks with every other word as he pleads. "Listen! I know you're upset. But... but we can make this right. What do you want? I'll get it."

Scarfoli's smile widens a bit more. "To watch you die."

"It's ready now, Mr. Scarfoli," Fugazzi says.

Scarfoli nods at his minion, then looks at Doyle. "Enjoy your journey, Mr. Donovan. I know I will." He reaches for the button, just as Mumbles enters with Max at gunpoint.

Max scans the room. He sees Scarfoli with the IV drip in his hand and does the math. A default resolution to buy some time comes out of his mouth. "Hold it!"

It works for the moment, and Scarfoli freezes. He stares at Max and cocks his head. "Who are you!?"

"He's Detective Lieutenant Max Tyrell, SFPD." Doyle says it with a sense of sudden pride and relief.

"Well," Scarfoli says. "You're a dead man, Max Tyrell."

Max steps forward, slowly, cautiously. "Listen... Doyle Donovan's been under my skin for sixteen years. I'll give you a thousand dollars if you let me push that button. Then you can do me."

Scarfoli shakes his head. "Sorry, but I've been looking forward to this all day." His thumb goes for the button again.

Max takes another step forward, quicker this time. "Grant a dead man his last wish. Ten thousand."

Scarfoli chuckles. "In today's economy, ten-thousand dollars is... well, it's ten-thousand dollars!"

Max inches closer still. "So, you gonna keep shootin' your mouth off or we gonna do some business?"

Scarfoli sizes Max up, smirks. "I don't see how I can refuse. He's all yours, dead man."

Max shakes his head through a quiet grumble, takes out his checkbook, and starts writing. The writing is barely legible because his eyes are on the needle. He's measuring. Calculating the next move. He bites deep into his cigar.

Fugazzi leans down into Doyle's ear. "He must really hate you."

"Nah." Doyle says. "He's just mad 'cause of all those times he arrested me."

Mumbles perks up. "He b-b-busted you?"

"Seven times." Doyle does his best to hold up seven digits while being restrained.

"Yeah. And his slimeball lawyer got the charges dropped. Every time," Max says.

Scarfoli and his two lackeys look at Doyle quizzically.

Doyle shrugs. "Lack of evidence. I got his number, if you want."

Max finishes writing the check and rips it out. He closes the rest of the distance between him and Scarfoli and hands the check over. Scarfoli looks at it, grins, then pockets it. Max sidles up to the embalming table and reaches for the button that separates Doyle from the afterlife. All eyes are on the button, when Max puts into action every movement he'd just planned.

He swings his arm around and grabs Scarfoli, putting him in a chokehold, using him as a shield. With his free hand, he quickly yanks the needle from Doyle's arm, ripping it out from under the tape. Doyle lets out a squeal, and Scarfoli gasps as the needle is buried into his throat. Max grabs the drip cord, and hovers his thumb over the button. "Put your guns in the sink and grab air, boys."

Mumbles and Fugazzi stand stunned and confused, their guns trained on Max.

Calmly, with fear in his eyes, Scarfoli says, "Do what the lawman says."

The men comply and put their guns in the sink and their hands in the air.

Scarfoli nods at Doyle. "Mumbles... cut the putz loose."

Reluctantly, Mumbles unbuckles the leather restraints, then backs away. Doyle sits up with a cocky smile and heads to the sink. He pulls out the two guns inside and aims one at Mumbles and the other at Fugazzi, then backs up next to Max.

Max yanks the needle out of Sacarfoli's neck, takes his own gun out of Doyle's hand and points it at Scarfoli.

Scarfoli puts a hand to his neck and lets out a quiet sigh of relief. "I'll take that phone number now."

But Max isn't done yet. He grabs Scarfoli's throat and starts squeezing. "Can it, dirtbag! Now, did you snatch our granddaughter?"

Scarfoli chokes out a chuckle and points at Doyle. "This lowlife has a family!?"

"Matter of opinion." Max strengthens his hold and pokes his gun into Scarfoli's ribs. "Tell me where she is."

"I don't know anything about her," Scarfoli says with a strained voice.

Max grits his teeth. "Wrong answer." His grip strengthens still. "You'd better make me believe you."

Scarfoli stretches his neck, trying to get relief. "Doyle Donovan's hustling my mamma. There's no return on ransoming a hostage from that deadbeat."

It's believable. Max has never seen an ounce of integrity in the man. He's a turnip you could never get blood from, no matter the muscle behind it. "If your hands are the least bit dirty, I'm gonna cut your fingers off one by one, then shoot you in the most painful places." Max lets go of Scarfoli, shoving him against the wall.

Doyle shakes his head. "Knew you wouldn't push the button."

"I'm already starting to regret it." Max takes out his phone and calls Delgado.

EIGHTEEN

MAX AND DOYLE watch Delgado do his thing through the two-way mirror. He's pacing in front of Scarfoli, Fugazzi, and Mumbles, who sit at the table in the interrogation room—three gazelle in the lion's den.

Max chews his unlit cigar, wishing he could be in that room, roughing them up, laying down the law. Behind this mirror, he feels helpless, useless. There's nothing he can do but watch, hoping Delgado's interrogation is adequate. If it's not, he'll have to break some rules. And some bones.

Doyle sidles up next to him, brotherly. "I always wanted to be the bad cop."

The door opens, and Delgado enters from the interrogation room. "Scarfoli's not sayin' another word 'til his momma gets here. But I don't think he snatched Talulah." He turns to Doyle. "Scarfoli and his thugs are third strikers. Once you sign your statement, we got 'em by the balls." He clenches a fist as though demonstrating the crushing of said balls. "Have you had any calls or contact with Talulah?"

Doyle shakes his head. "Nope. I'd tell ya if I did."

"No ransom demands? No word from anybody?"

"Listen... this ain't 'cause of me," Doyle says. "It's the

Chinese tough guys the skaters ratted out. They told us one had a scar across his face, and the other one was a hulk with tats on his scalp." Doyle nudges Max. "Tell him."

Max speaks up. "That's actually true. Cosmo's co-workers gave us descriptions."

Delgado's eyebrows shoot north. "You're just telling me this now?"

Doyle trades glances with Max. "We had a slight problem with coordinating transportation–"

"And then there was the thing with The Mortician–" Max added.

"But after that, we came straight here," Doyle says in his appeal for credibility.

Delgado holds a hand up to Doyle. "Wait here and zip it. The ADA will meet you. She's on her way now." He looks to Max. "C'mon, Max. The cruise ship security footage just got here. The FBI hand delivered it."

Max eyes turn to slits. "The FBI doesn't share squat. They only care about their issue. There must be a dual interest here."

"It just so happens their interest is Chinese crooks."

NINETEEN

DELGADO AND MAX walk through the door to Delgado's office. One of two chairs in front of the desk is filled with a fifty-something woman exhibiting the posture of a fence post, dressed in a navy-blue pantsuit.

Delgado extends an arm. "Max, this is FBI Field Agent Judith Quick. She brought over the cruise footage of the incident."

Judith stands and offers Max a hearty handshake. "It's a pleasure."

"Cut the crap. What do you want?" Max and his usual bedside manner.

The agent looks Max up and down, then seems to brush his attitude off. She taps the spacebar on a laptop which rests on the edge of Delgado's desk. A silent video plays. "Watch this," she says.

Max chomps his cigar, and his brows deepen the crease between them as he focuses on the screen. The ever-present cat sits on the desk. Delgado reaches out and pets it.

On the screen is black and white footage of Cosmo and Susan, Max's daughter, as they greet a passing couple in a cruise ship corridor. They're then followed by two men, who ignore the couple and suspiciously hide their faces from the camera. The time stamp on the screen says 2:00 AM. The top deck is deserted. A door opens. Cosmo and Susan step through, and immediately black hoods are slipped over their heads, and in a violent altercation their hands are cuffed behind their backs.

Max's nostrils flare. "How high?"

"Fourteenth deck. Sixteen stories," Agent Quick says.

Max swings a fist at a nearby filing cabinet. It booms throughout the office, startling the cat and leaving a dent in the metal cabinet. "Cheese and crackers!"

"I'll put a BOLO out for Talulah," Delgado says. "And keep an eye in the sky."

Their focus lands back on the screen, where Cosmo and Susan are being shoved past a dark figure standing motionless in the shadows. The figure is blurred and grainy. No identifying features. Near the safety rail of the deck, two men lift Cosmo and Susan, then move forward out of line of sight of the camera.

"From this angle, we can't actually see them go overboard," Agent Quick says.

Max chomps on his cigar. "How many of the cruise ship's security cameras had line of sight?"

"These aren't from the cruise ship. These are FBI cameras. We'd already had the ship under surveillance."

The video continues to play, and the shadowy figure flips open a Zippo. The fire illuminates the tattooed head of Xhing. He lights a thin cigar and glances at the camera with a smug expression, as though he knows he's being watched and finds it amusing. He snaps the Zippo shut and walks out of frame.

Agent Quick points at the screen. "What does this man want with the daughter of a retiree, whose reputation echoes through the bowels of this station?"

Delgado, with hands on his hips, says to the agent, "Want to share intel? You go first."

Agent Quick nods. "Okay... This ape works for the Counterfeit Ring King. Interpol's been wanting him for years. Now I'm spearheading a new task force, working with them and several other law enforcement agencies. We're going to nail this deplorable."

"Okay... then the SFPD wants a seat at the table."

"Done."

Delgado turns to Max. "Go ahead. Share."

Max eyes Quick. "They're not after my daughter. They're after her baby daddy."

Quick tilts her head. "Seriously? We took a look at that loser and immediately ruled him out."

Max is thankful Doyle isn't here. This is where he'd make things even more difficult, lashing out in defense of his son, who up until today Max never had an ounce of respect for. "A natural mistake. Happens to the best of us. But to everyone's surprise, Cosmo actually invented something worth a lot of money."

"Details," Quick demands.

"Some computer gadget on a skateboard. The better mouse trap."

"Roger that." Quick looks down, seems to contemplate the new information. "I think I got what I need. The video's a copy. You can keep it. If these people contact you about your granddaughter, let me know." Another round of handshakes. "We'll be in touch."

"Thanks," Delgado offers.

On her way out, Agent Quick has one last thought and turns back. "Delgado? A real hero doesn't wait for back-up." And with that, she makes her exit.

Inside, Max beams from the recognition, but there's no time to gloat. He springs into action, slamming a hand on

Delgado's desk. "Let's request the ship's manifest to get names for all the passengers and talk to the ship's security."

"They're already on their way here. I'm putting all our resources on this."

"I want in on the interviews."

Delgado shakes his head. "It's not your game anymore. But I'll keep you in the loop. Every step of the way."

Max points a stiff finger at the lieutenant. "You're not cutting me out, Delgado."

"Are you hearing me? You're retired!"

Max's cigar breaks off in his mouth and falls to the floor. His teeth grind what's left, before spitting it out. He takes a deep breath, ready with a mouthful of retaliation, then turns and leaves.

TWENTY

NICK SCARFOLI, Fugazzi, and Mumbles sit handcuffed in the interrogation room, a two-way mirror covering most of one wall. On the other side of the table, their lawyer, Willy Ambrose, ruffles papers in between brushing back the greasy product in his gray hair. Next to him sits Lydia, mascara heavy as ever. Doyle walks in with an assistant district attorney, who wears her hair in a tight ponytail. A pair of metal bracelets jingle when she moves her arm.

"Willy Ambrose," Doyle says. "How's business?"

"Same old. Same old."

"Is this the s-s-slimeball lawyer?" Mumbles stutters.

Doyle nods, and relief seems to wash over Mumbles, while Fugazzi giggles. Lydia winks a giant lash at Doyle and blows him a kiss. He smiles, and Nick lets out a disgusted sigh.

"Lydia. You look ravishing," Doyle says.

"Cara mia. How nice to see you." She holds her hands in a gesture of prayer, her eyes pleading with Doyle, as though silently begging for mercy. Or a favor.

Nick Scarfoli slams a hand down on the table. "Mamma! Quit flirting! Do something!"

Lydia gives Doyle another quick wink, and he nods in agreement. The favor granted in silence. "I just did," she says, then nods to Ambrose she has made a deal.

Ambrose turns to the ADA. "You've got no case, Miss Assistant District Attorney."

"Quite the opposite, actually," Ponytail says, while clicking a pen. "Doyle's testimony will finally put Nick Scarfoli *and* his gang behind bars."

Doyle's brow furrows as he feigns confusion. "Testify? About what? Against who?"

"Them! Who do you think?!"

"Max Tyrell paid these fine people to work for him," Ambrose says, producing the check Max had written to Scarfoli. "We're suing the city for the false arrest of Mr. Nick Scarfoli and his colleagues due to lack of evidence."

Fugazzi giggles again, as he exchanges a knowing look with Mumbles.

Lydia holds up an index finger. "Agente. I'd like to speak with Doyle... in privato, per favore."

Ponytail nods, and Doyle takes Lydia's arm, helping her out of the chair.

"What're you gonna do with my mamma?" Scarfoli asks.

Doyle opens the door to the interrogation room and starts to escort the older woman from the room. On the way out, he reaches over and snatches Max's check from Ambrose's grip, pockets it, then looks to Scarfoli. "Discuss the terms of your bail."

Lydia and Doyle walk down the hall of the police station, the click of her heels bouncing off the walls. "I had no idea what my son was up to. Please believe me, Doyle." Her grip on his arm tightens, as if to emphasize her innocence.

Doyle pats her arm. "I do. But, now your son owes me. It's a very heavy marker. One that I will call."

The gray curl on the side of Lydia's face bounces, as she nods in agreement. "A favor is a favor. You have my word. My Nicky's never welched on a marker in his life."

Max and Delgado catch up with them in the hall. Delgado feels the brush of the cat against his leg and looks down, suddenly realizing he still holds the leash. He hands the leash to Max. "I love the cat, Max. But it has to go."

Max, with a fresh, unlit cigar in his mouth, takes the leash and offers it to Lydia. "Want a cat?"

"Bellissimo!" Every tooth behind her lips is revealed through a smile that pushes her crows' feet back to her ears. "You've just made me an offer I cannot refuse." She takes the leash and picks up the cat, cradling it.

"We still on for tomorrow?" Doyle asks her.

Lydia shakes her head. "Sorry, Professor. Emma won two tickets to the fireworks show at Oracle Park in a radio contest."

Delgado chimes in. "Yeah, I heard they're setting off a trailer's worth of explosives every night this week."

Max scrunches his face, stuck on one particular word he heard. "Wait..." He holds a hand up. "Professor?"

Doyle shakes his head. "Don't ask."

TWENTY-ONE

IN CHINA TOWN, the roads are lit by open storefronts and hanging paper lanterns. People crowd the sidewalks with shopping bags in hand, while an SFPD helicopter hovers overhead, its searchlights crisscrossing the city's streets. Max's Cressida is parked in front of a small neighborhood cafe, above the door is a sign written in Chinese. Doyle and Max are inside, sitting in a booth with a variety of Chinese dishes in front of them, surrounded by discarded fortune cookies.

Max re-loads his piece, each bullet a quiet click under the table. "Rosie said they're running girls out of a dry cleaner here in China Town. We'll need to work the streets."

"Delgado said you were sidelined." Doyle finishes the sentence with a pair of chopsticks in his mouth.

"I'm not gonna sit here and let my street cred go to waste, twiddling my thumbs, waiting for the police." Max takes out a photo of himself and Talulah, pulls a knife from his boot, and begins cutting himself out of the photo. It's a picture of Talulah's first day of school this year. She's sporting a brand new backpack, new set of clothes, shoes.

Max himself sprung for the shoes. It's all she talked about that week, those shoes.

Doyle chews a mouthful of shrimp-fried rice. "Still go to confession every day?"

"Roger that."

"To have your sins forgiven?"

"That's the way it works. I'm always prepared to meet my maker."

Doyle wipes soy from his chin. "You ever think about dying?"

"You ever shut up? Here." Max hands the photo of Talulah to Doyle. "We're going to investigate. Show Talulah's picture around. I'll take one side of the street, you take the other."

"Got it. The 'Buddy system'. Watch each other's backs. Right, partner?"

Max searches Doyle's eyes, stares him down. He thinks Doyle would make a horrible cop. There's a very vain, very selfish bone nestled in the man. Putting him in a position that even remotely stinks of police work, or partnerdom, will be a test that Max is sure Doyle will fail. "A *real* cop has to trust his partner. Keep your eyes open for the ape with tattoos."

Max and Doyle spend the next few hours scouring every dry cleaner in China Town. Just as planned, Max takes one side of the street and Doyle the other. With each stop, they present photos of Talulah. No leads. Despite the ground covered and the open eye on civilians, they never see the man hiding in the shadows, watching them.

Max cranes his neck to inspect the large emblem above Chimera Dry Cleaners. He hasn't been in this one yet.

Before entering, he surveys the street for Doyle, or any character that may fit his description of suspicious, and again misses the man in the shadows.

Inside the dry cleaner, linen, bleach, and incense weave into a warm, clean scent. The muffled sound of industrial machinery and steam presses can be heard coming from the back. In the front, a young Chinese man with a buzz cut stands behind a counter, stapling a ticket.

Max shows him a photo of Talulah on his phone. "Have you seen this girl?"

The man looks at it. Studies it. He runs his hand across his scalp, and his lips squirm. "My memory not so good." He looks away from Max's phone.

Max considers the man's reaction. Was that a tell? There's something here. Max isn't sure if it's his own desperation after finding nothing all evening, or if there really was a sign that Buzz Cut is holding back important info. Something in his eyes. His body language. Even the smell of him. Is that sweat?

Max reaches into his pocket, urgently. Desperately. He pulls out a roll of cash and offers it to Buzz Cut. "Here. This should jog your memory. How about a guy with a scar on his face and a big ape with head tats?"

Buzz Cut eyes the cash, then snatches it, and shoves it in his pocket. His eyes dart from the service area to the street outside, searching. He leans in and whispers in a thick, Chinese accent, "In back. In private. Follow me."

The man leads Max down aisles of racked clothing, many of which are wrapped in plastic. A few women with hair tied back under bandanas, steam and iron pants and shirts. Another woman loads a giant machine full of clothes, as she pulls them from a four-wheeled canvas bin.

Once Max and Buzz Cut reach an area where clothing moves along a conveyer belt, Buzz makes a quick turn and pushes the hanging clothes into Max's face. Max shoves the clothes away and is quickly hit in the head with an iron. The old man reaches for his throbbing dome and stumbles back, while Buzz Cut drops the iron from his hand and catches Max by the coat. He pulls Max in and lifts him onto a hook, in the conveyor rack that moves the hanging clothes.

From the street, Doyle catches sight of Max through the two-story window, floating by his collar. Doyle makes eye contact with Max, hanging from the moving conveyor. Max's eyes plead for help, but before Doyle can even begin to form a plan, the man in the shadows steps forward. The man is sturdy, with skin like leather, and an Eastwood squint to his eye.

"Time to settle up, Doyle," the mystery man says.

Doyle jumps and turns, his heart a million BPMs. His eyes search for familiar features and finds them in the depth of the man's eyes. "Kenny Kings. How ya doin', pally?" Doyle's plastic smile fools no one. "Now's not a good time."

A fist appears out of the shadowy void and connects with Doyle's stomach. He staggers back and takes a knee. The stars come out, and his ears ring. By the time he's made sense of what happened, Kenny Kings has him in a headlock.

Doyle starts to pull a pleading spiel from the file he keeps for times like these and asks for specifics, before reciting the file's empty words. "Right... Okay, settle up for anything in particular?" He looks back across the street through the dry cleaner window and sees Max's eyes bulge from a screaming face, as he's carried away, up to the second floor.

Kenny speaks, "A twenty to one long shot, on a horse called—"

Doyle nods frantically, knowingly. "Johnson's Johnson."

"A horse you said could not lose."

Doyle pulls at Kenny's arm, giving his throat the room to swallow. "Got it straight from Big Ears."

"Well, it seems the horse developed colic."

Doyle strains under the man's arm as he tightens his hold, face turning red. "My most heartfelt sympathies."

"So, you owe me three hundred large."

Confused, Doyle squirms. "But... your wager was only fifteen G!"

"Correct." Kenny tightens all the more. "And at twenty to one odds, I lost three hundred large."

Doyle pulls at his arm again, harder this time. "Twenty to one. Of course, I hadn't... here." Doyle lets go and reaches into his pocket for Lydia's check. He finds it, pulls it out, and offers it with two shaky fingers. "A good faith deposit."

Kenny snatches the check and looks at it. *Made out to "CASH" for $1000.* "This ain't a deposit. It's an insult! You'll have the whole three hundred by Monday. Am I clear?"

"Crystal. I'll have it by Monday. On my dearly departed mother's honor."

He gives Doyle's neck one last squeeze, then lets go and disappears into the shadows from where he came.

♧

Wang Tzu leans over a glass table, studying a counterfeit $100 bill with an eye piece. He inspects every detail, making sure any irregularity in the watermark is subtle, that there's no color shift in the ink. Satisfied, he grins with a nod, and the phone rings. It's his nephew, calling from Chimera Dry Cleaners.

He picks up. "Greetings, nephew."

The tone of his nephew's voice is rushed and demands attention. Wang Tzu listens intently.

⬡

Buzz Cut speaks into the phone. "...and he knows something, Uncle. He described both you and Xhing." Max lies on the floor behind him, just a few feet away. His feet and hands are bound by duct tape, his mouth packed with a linen handkerchief, a piece of twine wrapped twice around his head, holding in the gag.

Through the phone, Wang Tzu says, "See if he has any I.D. on him."

Buzz Cut goes to Max, and rifles through his pockets. He removes his badge and ID. "His name is Maximillian Tyrell. He's a retired cop."

Wang Tzu tells his nephew to put the man on the phone. Buzz Cut complies, taking the gag from Max's mouth and holding the phone to his ear. Through the phone, Wang Tzu tells Max to work with them. He tells him he'll be rewarded.

"I'll have no part of your plan," Max replies, his lip curled in disgust.

"You're not listening," the voice in the phone says.

⬡

Wang Tzu stands in a large warehouse that has been kept meticulously clean. In the center of the area sit rows of large high-tech copiers spitting counterfeit bills, while workers

107

spread around tables bundle them in red wrappers stamped with Chimera's emblem.

"Now listen carefully." Wang Tzu speaks into the cell phone. Max's daughter Susan sits tied to an office chair, a bandana–being used as a gag–tied tightly around her mouth. Her eyes still hold the smudged remnants of weeks old mascara, adding to the sleepless circles of dark around them. Xhing stands next to her, statue still with his arms crossed. Susan belts out a muffled scream through the gag, and Wang Tzu pulls at it, allowing a brief, panic-filled declaration into the phone as it's held to her face. "Daddy! They have Talulah!"

The distorted crackle of Max through the phone, "Susan?!" You're alive!"

Wang Tzu puts the phone back to his own ear. "I assume I have your complete obedience now?"

"I'm sorry. I'm listening," Max says through the phone.

Wang Tzu's face splits with a smile. "That's good. This will all be over tomorrow night. Say nothing, or your family will suffer the consequences! Is that understood?"

"Yes. Just don't hurt anybody."

At the dry cleaners, Buzz Cut pulls the phone from Max's ear and speaks into it. "How many girls do you want me to bring you tonight, Uncle?"

Wang Tzu watches Susan as she squirms in the chair, helpless. "The usual. And... upon reflection... leave nothing to chance. Kill Maximillian Tyrell!"

"No!" Susan screams. "Please, no!" She glares defiantly at her captor, then spits at him. Wang Tzu nods to Xhing, who hits Susan hard in the face, drawing blood. The punch produces a rage-filled grunt of desperation from the far corner of the room, where Cosmo Donovan sits bound in his own chair, struggling against the restraining ropes.

Buzz Cut ends the call and quickly grabs a plastic, dry-cleaning bags from a box in the corner of the room. Next, the roll of duct tape he used to bind Max. He looks at his captive and shrugs, like he has no choice but to execute this next plan of action.

Max does the math and realizes what's coming next. "Hey, now! I just struck a deal with your uncle. I zip my lip and nobody gets hurt."

Buzz Cut ignores Max and puts the bag over his head, cinching it with the duct tape, cutting off any chance for oxygen.

"Hey, buster! Catch!" a voice behind him.

Doyle tosses a hot iron at the man, whose reflex—and mistake—is to catch it. The room fills with the sound of sizzling flesh and a grown man's yelp, while Max wriggles like a maggot with his bound limbs and plastic-cocooned head.

Doyle continues his attack with a can of starch, spraying it into Buzz Cut's face, then reaches for an open bottle of bleach. "Here... that'll get infected. Better keep it clean." Pouring the bleach onto the man's hot, blistering hands.

"Ahhhh!" Buzz Cut screams, lashing out blindly.

Doyle makes his finishing move by smashing Buzz Cut's head on a sink, snap-cracking the young man's nose, and out go the lights, as the beaten and burned man drops to the floor. Max bangs his legs against a cupboard, then lies still. The maggot dance is over, the bag around his head now fogged with dying breath. Doyle rushes to him, buries his fingers into the plastic and rips a hole through it, exposing Max's face, then rips the bag from his head. Next, he slaps the limp man's cheek, and Max gasps, his eyes fluttering.

Through gulping breaths, Max says, "We found the dirt bags, and now I'll nail 'em. Every one of 'em."

While Doyle tears away the tape from Max's wrists, Buzz Cut groans behind them, grabbing his head. After

Max's hands are free, he strips the tape from his legs and grabs Buzz Cut's phone. He dials *69. It comes back as restricted.

"Gimme a hand," Doyle says, as he pulls Buzz Cut by an ankle.

"Sure." Max slams the phone down on the Chinese man's head, knocking him out.

"Hey!" Doyle lets go of the ankle. "Now we can't make him talk."

"Beat this low-life to a pulp, he'll never talk." Max plants his GPS tracking device in Buzz Cuts pocket.

Doyle's face lightens. There's a smile there. "We make a good team, don't we, partner?"

Max rolls his eyes. "Until I decide not to."

TWENTY-TWO

IT'S A CLEAR NIGHT, and the bullet-ridden Cressida climbs San Francisco's streets. Max drives with his cell on the dash, Delgado on the other end. Doyle rides shotgun, eavesdropping on the call.

"I talked to Susan," Max says to the phone. "She's alive."

Doyle swivels his head and butts in. "Any news about Cosmo?"

Max shakes his head. "Buzz Cut called the other guy 'Xhing' when talking to his uncle. Told him we had descriptions, so one of these is the ape, the other is scarface."

"On it," Delgado through the phone. "I'll see what I can find."

"I'm gonna pick up some stuff, and then go back to sit on the dirtbag at the dry cleaners," Max says.

"Over my dead body!" Delgado yells.

Max can picture the vein in the middle of the lieutenant's forehead. He shrugs. "Have it your way. Suicide's a terrible thing."

"If you do me, make sure you hide the corpse. I've already got too much paperwork."

Max hits the blinker, makes a left turn. "After their deal tomorrow night, they'll kill everybody. You know that, right? The clock's ticking."

"Copy that," Delgado says. "But, Max... if you see or hear anything, you call it in. And you *wait* for backup."

♢

San Pedro, Chimera Corporation's Industrial Compound

Wang Tzu stands inside a warehouse with two mid-eastern men next to several wooden crates. Xhing lumbers nearby with a leather valise. A secret meeting. Any fly on the wall could sense the tension, the evil intent with the upcoming exchange. Wang Tzu nods, and the two men open the crates and display the contents. RPG rockets, AR-15s, M&P15 VTACs, and R-15 Carbines.

Wang Tzu looks to Xhing. He nods, and Xhing opens the bag. Stacks of $100-bills encased in red wrappers, stamped with Chimera's emblem.

"So?" Wang Tzu says. "Deal or no deal?"

The two middle-easterners take the valise and close it, then carry it to an immaculately clean SUV. The engine starts, and they drive off. The meeting is adjourned, uneventful.

Xhing and Wang Tzu trade glances and begin to laugh. With the means to print money, the sky's the limit. After heading upstairs, they enter the second-floor loft office, when their celebration is interrupted by the buzz of Wang Tzu's phone.

With the cheer still in his voice, he answers it. "Yes, nephew." He listens, and his face melts, the smile dripping into a frown. His brow pinches, his lip curls.

A timid and unnaturally nasally voice through the

phone tells Xhing how sorry he is, it wasn't his fault that Max got away. "He had a partner," Buzz Cut says.

Wang Tzu ends the call and turns to his friend. "Xhing. Go send a message."

On the other side of the room, Susan sits with terror in her eyes.

TWENTY-THREE

MAX'S lonely house on the hill. The trash cans remain on the curb, emptied. Cressida in the driveway. The warm glow of light through the living room window disguises the crumbling abode as something homey. It used to be, back when raising Susan. Back when her mother was still in the picture. But these days, he doesn't even have it in him to clear the cobwebs.

In the bedroom, Max loops his tie in the mirror. He's wearing his other cheap suit. The one that fits a little looser, hiding his love for diner food.

Doyle paces through the house, spots a fresh banana on the kitchen island and grabs it. "At your age," he says. "I guess you don't buy green bananas anymore."

"Sure I do." Max cinches the tie to his neck. "They make great enemas."

Doyle takes a bite of the fruit, looks over the photographs and commendations on the wall in the living room. Most pictures are either cut in half or have the faces of people torn out of them. "I'm hurt, Max. No pictures of me?"

Max takes a deep breath, silently shakes his head, ignoring the man.

"Who are all these headless people? You need help. Admit it."

"You can take your two cents and shove it where it belongs."

Doyle wanders over to the fireplace mantle and notes the two shadow boxes displayed over it. One is for Max, the other for his late father. Both hold pistols, handcuffs, badges, medals, decorations, and retired police memorabilia. Next to that is a framed grant deed. "You're a regular poster boy for the American dream, aren't ya?"

Max peeks around the corner, sees what Doyle's admiring. "I'd just paid off the mortgage, so I had the deed framed... behind indestructible museum glass."

Doyle sees the same photo that was hanging in Delgado's office, but in this one the head of the third cop has been cut out. Doyle shakes his head. "I heard you haven't spoken to your old partner in years. What's the story?"

After one last tug of the tie, Max walks into the living room and heads over to the sea chest behind the couch. He unlocks its childproof lock and lifts the lid. It's a weapons cache, with an intimidating arsenal inside. "You got diarrhea of the mouth."

Doyle wanders still, eyeing the rest of the photos until he comes upon one of Max's wedding. The bride has a messy circle of white paint blocking out her face. "That has to be your ex. She really must've rattled your cage."

Max looks up, glances at the photo. "She took all our money, left me with the mortgage and a daughter to raise on my own. What do you think?"

"Beautiful woman. Rest her soul."

Max reaches down into the sea chest, comes up holding

.50 caliber handgun and points it at Doyle's face, chambers a round.

Doyle tilts his head. "What is that thing? A cannon?"

Max's lip curls, and his eyes squint, like the urge to pull the trigger is growing stronger. The moment passes, and his face relaxes. He puts the gun in a canvas bag. "It's a Smith and Wesson fifty caliber magnum. One shot'll take an elephant down at a hundred yards."

Doyle squints his own eyes. "You could kill me and you wouldn't feel a thing, would you?"

Max reaches back into the chest, pulls out a revolver and starts loading it with ammo. "I'd feel something."

"Yeah? What?"

"I don't know. Maybe a slight kick, depending on which bullet I used." He offers Doyle the revolver. "Here. I've got a toy to share."

Doyle pushes the gun away. "I'd kill myself with that, partner."

The lip curl. The hatred in his eye. "My last *partner* ran off with my wife."

"*Ex*-wife."

"That's 'cause he ran off with her, Einstein."

Max packs the revolver in the canvas bag, heads to the fridge, and gets all the ammo from inside. He takes a quick swig of prune juice and packs the ammo in the bag, then heads for the front door. Doyle, done with the pictorial tour of Max's living room, follows him out the door.

"Didn't Delgado say you were supposed to wait for backup?" Doyle asks.

"You are my backup."

With his hand on the passenger side door, Doyle asks, "Do you need to *go* before we go?"

Max stops. Considers the question, then nods and heads back inside.

As they drive down the hill, away from Max's home, Doyle gives a low whistle. "You got a million dollar view from up here."

"Yeah, well you ever see an artsy-fartsy coffee shop open up in your neighborhood, make sure and kill it before it spreads."

"Must get lonely in a place this big."

"Not really," Max says.

"You ever think about remodeling?"

"Might add a bathroom. Never know."

"I know a guy does re-fi's. But you gotta cut down those hedges first." Doyle clocks an approaching caravan of construction vehicles and points them out. "Wonder where they're going."

The vehicles pass by, heading up the hill–an oversized truck, backhoe, and a crane. What Max and Doyle don't see is a grinning Xhing sitting in the bulldozer at the lead, as the procession heads straight for Max's house. Xhing smiles. It's evil.

⬡

The rest of the caravan stops in front of Max's house, while Xhing drives the bulldozer through the trashcans and straight into Max's living room. Accolades are thrown from the living room wall, as it begins to fold and splinter.

Neighbor Norm watches "Jeopardy" on his TV, reading the closed-captioned subtitles out loud, oblivious to the chaos next door. The television blares, while his hearing aids squeal on the end table.

TWENTY-FOUR

THE CRESSIDA SITS in the red zone in front of the San Francisco Police Station, bullet holes adorning its once smooth and rust-free exterior. Windshield demolished. Inside the station, Max and Doyle sit with Delgado, who is behind his desk and on the computer.

Delgado spins the monitor and shows his two visitors a mugshot, as well as the accompanying criminal record. "That's Xhing. The tchotchkes on his scalp list his kills. The Chinese mafia use enforcers like this for their illicit activities in auto theft, truck hijacking, corporate espionage, and counterfeiting."

Doyle lights up. "Did you say counterfeiting? That's outrageous!" He gives it more thought, curiosity in his eye. "So... how's that work?"

Before anyone can tell Doyle to forget it, the phone rings. Delgado grabs it. His face turns to stone, and his eyes dart to Max. "On our way."

○

Traffic pulls to the side as the Cressida speeds through, a police escort just ahead. Sirens and cherry-red lights. The phone call Delgado received can't possibly be true. There's been a mix up. But as they climb the hill, Max can already see his house is gone. Where he should have otherwise seen the crest of the attic window and the ancient antennae that hadn't worked in decades, there was only sky.

A single patrol car is on the scene when the rest arrive. Neighbors stand outside surveying the damage, confused and curious. Max parks, exits, his mouth agape at the leveling of his house, the absolute destruction. Where there once stood a house full of memories, only a crumpled shell remains, as though a tiny tornado swept through, touching only his residence—this one house and its photographs, its doorframe where a father measured his daughter's height through the years, and most recently, Talulah's safe haven. It's gone.

Doyle hesitates speaking, struggling to find the appropriate words. Finally, he breaks the ice. "Shame about your house. And you just paid off your mortgage."

Max closes his mouth, swallows through a dry throat. "This is a message. To make a point. For everyone to see."

Doyle spins around, looks at San Francisco and its winding streets. "All I see is a great view. The Chinese did you a favor tearin' down all those overgrown hedges."

Delgado speaks. "They want Max to stay out of their business and keep quiet."

Doyle, feeling sympathetic, pats Max's shoulder. "C'mon. You can crash at my place."

"I don't need sleep. I need a plan."

Delgado raises a finger at Max. "Do *not* make me put an ankle bracelet on you. Because I will. I mean it, Max."

Doyle pulls at Max's shoulder, trying to lead him away

from the ugly sight. "I do my best planning after a few shots of tequila and some canoodle."

Max pulls away and wanders to the wreckage, his ears shut to the voices behind him. He stands where the living room used to be and kicks some of the rubble around, searching for anything that resembles home. The grant deed peeks out from under a chunk of plaster. The frame is barely held together, the glass intact. Once again, Max swallows hard. "A drink sounds good right now."

Delgado approaches Max and puts an arm around him, grips his shoulder tight and slips a GPS tracker into his jacket pocket—the same kind Max used. "Stay safe, brother. You need me. You call."

Max seems to break from a trance. The somber meditation has cleared his head and given him focus. There's only one goal to obtain: get his children back. And there's only one way to obtain that goal: take down these scumbags. Home or no home, his heart is with family, who need him now more than ever.

Max turns and walks back to the Cressida, Doyle following behind. The two get in the car, and Delgado watches them pull away. He takes his cellphone out, opens the tracking app, and watches the blinking light as it heads down the hill.

TWENTY-FIVE

A VAN SQUEALS into Wang Tzu's warehouse. The brakes slam, and Buzz Cut gets out, his hands cocooned in gauze from that game of catch with the iron. A bandage on his nose. Two scantily clad women step out. To mistake them for anything but prostitutes would be ignorant—the gartered, showy legs and the way they pivot says it all. Workers inside the warehouse swarm the van, while Wang Tzu stands from a table nearby. With his head down, Buzz Cut walks to him and hands him a satchel. "I'm sorry, Uncle."

Wang Tzu takes the satchel and opens it. It's packed full of one-dollar bills. He nods, closes the satchel, then walks to a stairway leading up, while the prostitutes start to dance for any worker who cares to watch, captivating them with an entrancingly slow swing of their hips.

○

Max and Doyle pull into Paradise Village. A banner above the entrance reads *Rosie's Boylesque Revue Tonight!* in giant, glittery letters. The Cressida doors open, and the usual squeaky creak is replaced by a deep groan due to the recent onslaught of bullets having pummeled the car's innards.

"...so, that's just me spitballing. But what do you think?" Doyle shuts the hole-riddled passenger door.

"I think you left out the part about the way to get us in—"

"No problem... if you can kidnap a Chinaman and steal a van."

Max nods. "Not a problem."

From across the parking lot, Tommy Minetti and three musclebound thugs spot Doyle before he sees them. Minetti points a stiff finger, and his face burns red. "Doyle Donovan! I'm gonna kill you!"

Doyle and Max swivel their heads. In unison, "*That's* a problem!"

Minetti's gun is out in the blink of an eye. Another blink, and a bullet is on the loose. It blasts into the Cressida's driver's side door. Max and Doyle make a beeline to a nearby shuttle van and dive for cover. Max growls with pain as his knee hits the pavement. Doyle ducks his head between his knees. Another bullet flies, zipping past them. Max pulls his gun, peeks across the hood of the van and returns fire with two shots of his own. Minetti's men add their own bullets to the barrage, and the shuttle van absorbs them all.

Max pulls the gun back and clutches it to his chest. "I've got two shots left!"

"What?!" Doyle yells over the gunfire. "You packed all that ammo!"

"It's in the car." They both look at the Cressida. It may as well be a hundred miles away. "We stay here, we're Swiss cheese." A window in the shuttle van shatters. A tire pops, and the van lowers. "On my signal. Go!"

The two pop up from behind the shuttle, and Max fires

his last two bullets, as they sprint into the shadows, creeping along a few parked cars, until they reach a converted school bus painted a rainbow of bright colors. Written on the side are the words *Rosie's Boylesque Revue!*

From somewhere on the other side of the street, Minetti calls out, "Find them!" Then the sound of scurrying footsteps in different directions, as the men spread out and begin their search.

Max and Doyle flatten against the school bus and quietly move alongside it, until they reach the door. Doyle pushes Max in through the door, who falls on the steps leading inside. Another bang to his knee. He grits his teeth through the pain and silently promises to pay Doyle back for it, if they make it through this.

Inside the bus, it's brightly lit. The complete reconstruction of the interior shows the seats have been pulled and replaced with vanities, complete with mirrors—a dressing room on wheels. A slew of female impersonators in their sequined dresses are peeking through the windows, curious about the chaos outside.

All is quiet inside, as the footsteps outside grow louder. And it's clear to everyone that Max and Doyle are in desperate need of sanctuary as they freeze in position, listening intently to Minetti's men as they pass by the bus.

Finally, Doyle climbs over Max and crawls to the middle of the bus. "Rosie. We need your help."

Rosie, unshaken by events, strolls down the aisle, checking on the drag queens, then reaches Doyle. "By all means, sweetie. You look exhausted. You should sit down." Rosie points to a single booth seat toward the back.

Max picks himself up off the stairs. "I'm not staying here!" he says a little too loud.

"You're an adult now, Max. You can do whatever you want." Doyle says.

Max looks out the window, sees Minetti's men patrolling the area, guns out. "I wanna pee," he says.

"Right in there." Rosie points to what looks like a standing closet at the back of the bus.

Max squeezes through the crowd of drag queens, some of whom have returned to their makeup stations, donning their wigs, applying fake lashes, and zipping dresses. He reaches the bathroom and heads inside.

○

Minetti's men continue their search—down alleys, behind vehicles, on fire escapes, and in Dumpsters. With no sign of their targets, the men regroup in front of Rosie's bus, when the construction of their next plan is interrupted by the opening of the bus door, as Rosie's revue begin to file out in all their glittery and sequined glory.

Before the bus is empty, Minetti's men squeeze through the parade of drag queens and enter the bus, searching each seat and pushing past the last two queens in the flamboyant row to check the bathroom. Empty.

As the end of the line files out of the bus, the last queen covers his knee brace with an unruly skirt, and limps down the bus steps. Doyle—also in drag—whispers to his cross-dressing friend, "Keep your cool, partner. Keep your cool."

Inside Paradise Village, an elderly couple shuffling on walkers, approach a bouncer seated on a stool in front of the Community Room, a clipboard in his hand. The couple flash their resident passes, and the bouncer points to a sign on the wall next to him that reads *Performers Only*. Disappointed, the couple walk away, passing Tommy Minetti and his minions, who approach the bouncer.

"We're looking for Doyle Donovan," Minetti folds a

124

hundred-dollar bill into the bouncer's hand, while the female impersonators form a line nearby.

The bouncer pockets the money. "Haven't seen him," he says. "And don't worry. Doyle Donovan won't get by me." He stands and removes a velvet rope blocking the entrance backstage. "Now, excuse me, fellas." He turns to the line of queens and nods. "Hi, girls." And waves them in. "Right this way, ladies."

The line of sequined men pass through and head backstage, while Minetti gives them all a once over. In the back, Max and Doyle step out of the line, intent on escaping, then immediately fall back in when they see Minetti standing there, blocking their escape. With no other choice, they walk past the bouncer and follow the line ahead.

The bouncer hooks the velvet rope, closing off the entrance, and Minetti points to his thugs. "My friends and I... we'd like to hang around, just in case he shows up."

The bouncer gives a light shrug that says, *whatever you gotta do.*

Meanwhile, Rosie and her revue make their way backstage, palms down, hips swinging, lashes flittering—the exaggerated body language of women they've practiced for years. Max and Doyle finally drop from the line and sweep the room, desperate for a way out. Max goes for a door, turns the knob. Locked.

"Look." Doyle points toward the backstage entrance, where Minetti stands with his hoods, giving them instructions. No getting through there.

Emma Schlumburger has traded her feather boa in for a clipboard and is stage managing the show, inspecting each glittery gown and teased wig, offering compliments along the way. She reaches Max and gives him a pat on his rear end. "Well, aren't you a cutie pie."

Max bats her hand away and scurries up to Doyle, whispers, "I can't do this."

Doyle spots another door toward the head of the line and pulls Max with him. A quick run brings them to the far side of the room, and they go for the door.

Locked.

There's no way out. Music swells from somewhere, and the crowd beyond the curtain begins to hush. An upcoming horror awaits. Unimaginable embarrassment. For Max, taking a bullet seems like the most logical–and honorable– choice. But Rosie snatches him by the arm. She's so far up in his face he can smell her lip gloss. "Okay, Tootsie. Stay in the back. Screw up my show, your ass is mine!"

Emma throws her hands up, each finger tipped with bright-red polish. "Places, everyone. Places!"

By the backstage entrance, Minetti points at the crowd, and his two minions head into the audience, walking past Lydia, who sits unaware and smiling in an aisle seat in the front row.

Emma smooths out her dress and walks to the center of the stage, where a microphone stands head high. "And here's the moment we've been waiting for. Make some noise for Rosie and her Boylesque Revue!"

The crowd applauds, and a few whistles echo through the auditorium, while Minetti's men continue their patrol through the aisles, searching. Loud, bassy R&B music is queued, and the female impersonators strut out onto the stage in exaggerated fashion. Hips bouncing. Stage light twinkling off from every shiny dress.

Max and Doyle, clearly the odd men out, head for a small set of stairs that lead off the stage, but the sight of Minetti's men among the crowd forces them back into position.

Rosie, with a howling falsetto, begins to sing along with

the roaring soundtrack, while the swaying men start their choreographed dance. The line suddenly breaks, leaving Max behind, and Rosie shoots him a dirty look. Doyle quickly grabs Max and spins him around, bringing him back into formation. Max's eyes are anywhere but the stage, frantically searching for a way out, when he makes eye contact with Minetti, who seems oblivious to his disguise. Instead, he offers a wave and a smile. The rest of the line continue their dance, turn and bend over, waving their butts at the audience.

Finally, following Doyle's lead, Max gives in and starts to dance, giving it everything he's got and doing his best to blend in. He watches the others, mimicking them with slight delay and following every move, kicking out with his bad knee and biting back the pain. He swings his head back, nearly losing his wig, but holds it on with a quick hand.

The hoods have taken to enjoying the show with eyes glued to the entertainment. Max looks to his left and to his right, being careful to continue mimicking the other dancers' moves. He brings his arm up, and his wristwatch catches on his wig, yanking it from his head. Minetti seems to catch the mishap and squints suspiciously at Max.

Doyle sees the rogue wig, and pulls it back to Max's head. But with the watch still attached, Max's arm is brought with it like a marionette on strings. He yanks his arm away, and the wig flies off the stage, landing on a front-row patron.

While the dance continues, Minetti pulls a .45 from inside his blazer, conceals it, and moves to the side-stage curtain. Max attempts another quick turn to keep in line, and his knee gives out, forcing his weight into Doyle. Doyle falls at the edge of the stage, rolls off, and lands at the feet of Lydia Scarfoli with his face in her lap. He looks up, whispers, "Lydia. It's me. Doyle."

"You playing for both teams now?" she asks him.

Gun fire explodes as the two thugs unload, then Minetti adds to the chaos with his own gun. People duck, fall, and slither from their seats. The dancers scurry. Max slides off the three-foot stage and joins Doyle in the front. A sleeping man in the back row doesn't move a muscle.

The double doors at the head of the auditorium burst open, and the bouncer rushes in, puffed chest and ready for battle. He sprints to the pane of emergency glass along the wall, smashes it with an elbow, and pulls out the fire hose inside. With a single twist of a valve, water shoots from the hose, as the bouncer aims from the hip toward Minetti and his men. "We have a strict No-Guns-Allowed policy here. Everybody out!"

Doyle grabs Lydia by the hand. "C'mon, Toots! Time to split!" He turns to find Max behind him, snatches his hand too, and starts to run.

Emma runs behind Max and puts a hand on his back. "I'm on your six!," she says as they run to safety back stage, while a horizontal geyser takes down its armed targets behind them.

⛉

At daybreak, Neighbor Norm walks to the street, picks up his waiting copy of The Daily News, and shakes it open. Before he reads a word, the empty space to his right where a house once stood catches his eye. Max's house is leveled. Norm drops the paper. The headline:

COUNTERFEIT RING KING, FBI'S MOST
WANTED

TWENTY-SIX

AT PARADISE VILLAGE, the sun begins its climb, painting the trees a golden amber. Birds chirp peacefully, and the flowers planted in surrounding beds along the building sway subtly in the early-morning breeze. A postcard perfect break of day.

Inside Lydia's room, Doyle mutters to himself, "My kingdom for a camera," as he watches Max sleep on the bed. Max is wearing a pink boa and a stupid grin. Emma Schlumburger lies next to him, her hands bound to the headboard by nylon stockings.

Doyle weaves through the obstacle course of tequila bottles and stripped clothing, then sits in a chair in front of a mirror, dips two fingers into an open container of cold cream and spreads it around his face. He rubs at the goo with a tissue, removing last night's gaudy makeup.

The still-unnamed cat strolls through the room, then jumps on Max's head, stirring him awake. When Max opens his eyes, he's staring into Emma's mascara-smeared face.

"This really was an affair to remember, darling," she says with a sly grin.

Max sits up like the bed's on fire. "Uhh... Doyle?! Who is this?"

Doyle swings around, his face a muddied mess of cream, eyeliner, and too much blush. "You weren't properly introduced last night, were you? Emma, meet Detective Maximilian Tyrell. Active duty. *Very* active." He gets up–sporting a red teddy–and begins to untie Emma from the bed's headboard.

"You're a cop?" Emma asks. "Where are your handcuffs? We could have used 'em last night."

Max collapses, slamming the back of his head on the pillow. "Shoot me now."

Emma massages her wrists. "Hey, Lydia!"

Lydia pops out from under the covers, and Emma nods at how the blanket pokes up at Max's lower half. "Look at this! Morning wood!"

Lydia ducks back under the covers to confirm, and Max frantically grabs at the boa around his neck, trying to cover himself.

Doyle picks up an empty bottle of Viagra off the floor. "Hey, Sir Lance-a-Lot. You were only supposed to take one."

Lydia peeks under the covers again. "I like your tattoo."

"Did you tattoo your address in case you can't remember where you live?" Doyle hands Max the cold cream and a tissue.

Max sits back up, puts the pillow on his lap. He takes the cold cream, starts applying it with all the finesse of a four-year-old. "My tattoo is none of your business."

Emma turns to Doyle. "You should see where it is. What does FUBAR mean?"

⬡

After cleaning up and delivering some awkward goodbyes, Max and Doyle head to the Cressida. They pass a group of Paradise Village residents doing tai chi on a manicured patch of grass. Doyle eyes one of the women as she stretches her arms. "You're doing me proud, Snoopy," he says to Max. "I have a certain reputation to maintain around here."

Max's head is down, eyeing the pavement in a walk of shame. He's all business. "Yeah, well as soon as we rescue Talulah, I'm gonna kill you."

"You're worse than my late wife. All she ever did was complain." Doyle spots a vacancy sign for the village. "Hey, look. There's a vacancy. Ya know... two smokin' hot sisters just moved in. You should, too. I can introduce ya."

"Not interested."

"But, Max, they're from Slovenia. All they've ever been taught, their whole lives, is how to please men."

Max opens the driver's side door of his car. "Slovenia, huh? Why didn't you say so? Set me up."

"Yeah?! When?"

"When I'm dead." Max gets in the car.

Doyle opens the passenger door. "Why wait? You're already in a coma."

Max sticks the key into the ignition and starts the car. They pull out of the parking lot, and Doyle throws a wave at the tai chi women. Wind rushes through the car where the windshield used to be, burning their eyes. Max squints, blinking often, while Doyle throws on a pair of shades.

"We need to find out where Buzz Cut takes the girls," Doyle says, then gets distracted. "You could eat a bug driving like this, ya know? Thing could fly right between your teeth, get rammed right in there."

"Bugs are full of protein. Suck it up." Max points to his phone mounted on his dash. The GPS app is open and a dot blinking on a map. "As far as Buzz Cut, I put a GPS on that worthless piece of human garbage."

"What are we gonna do, stake him out?"

Max lets a smile spill across his face.

○

Inside the parked Cressida, Max chomps on his unlit cigar and views the Chimera compound through a pair of binoculars. The place is large, with a mountainous gate. Armed sentries patrol behind a high-voltage security fence. They look attentive, ready for anything.

While waiting for his turn with the binoculars, Doyle stares at the cigar jutting from Max's mouth. "You ever light that thing?"

"Smoking's bad for your health."

"So is eating cigars."

Max pulls the binocs away from his eyes. "It's a fortress. This'll have to be a SWAT callout."

Doyle stares off, appearing to imagine such a scenario. "Have SWAT storm a compound? What could possibly go wrong?" He drops the trance and swivels to Max. "Are you crazy?! Did you forget what happened in Waco?! Ruby Ridge?! Our kids are in there! And *I'm* going to rescue them." He points to his own chest. "Not any SWAT team, with their grappling hook-wearing, window-crashing ninja suits. I'll do it with or without your help. And if you *don't* help, I'll *kill* you!" Doyle snatches the binocs and holds them up to his eyes, scoping out the Chimera compound.

Max grabs a sandwich from a large paper bag full of stake-out food: more sandwiches, two bananas, and potato chips.

With the radio playing jazz on the lowest setting, Max

unwraps the sandwich and takes a bite, sits back in his seat and works the problem. "We call Delgado, we'll be cut out. We got a way in… if I steal a van and kidnap a chinaman. But then what?"

Through the binocs, Doyle spots Hawk Eye and Two Fingers in the cab of an eighteen-wheel rig. The truck stops at the guard kiosk, and an armed sentry opens the security gate, then waves them in. Doyle sets the binocs down long enough to grab himself a sandwich. "Listen, partner. I want you to sit there and admire me for a while. 'Cause I just got an idea for a plan." Doyle shakes his head in admiration. "I don't know how I do it."

♧

Inside the Chimera compound, there's a beehive of activity in the spacious layout. Armed guards patrolling. Workers unloading racks of stolen goods. In the far corner is a chop shop—a welder focused on his assignment, a shower of sparks illuminating the corner bright orange.

The eighteen-wheeler rolls to a stop, and the air brakes hiss. Hawk Eye and Two Fingers hop out, and Wang Tzu approaches, with Xhing close behind.

"We got porcelain ponies tonight!" Hawk Eye says, placing a finger under his eyepatch and scratching a deep itch.

Wang Tzu shakes his head. "No place for ponies."

"They're toilets, not horses. Fifteen hundred crappers," Two Fingers adds.

"I'll give you ten thousand." Wang Tzu's stoneface tells the man he'll not get a penny more.

"You got a deal." Hawk Eye extends a hand that goes ignored.

Xhing scribbles something on a pad of paper, rips it out,

133

nods towards his first-floor office, and hands Hawk Eye the voucher.

"Next time," Wang Tzu glares at his subservient's one good eye. "Bring me cars or cigarettes. We make more money."

○

Max parks the Cressida at Oracle Park, squints his eyes against the sun, and steps out.

Doyle follows his lead, stands up, fixes his pant leg, adjusts himself. "Now I understand why you didn't wait for backup, back in the day."

"You're singing to the choir." Max shuts his door.

Doyle shuts his. "What was it that day? Family?"

"School bus full of kids."

Doyle shakes an empathetic head. "Shoulda got a medal."

"It was in my house."

Doyle nods his head and lets the troubling words hang, as he follows Max to Oracle Park's ticket office, where the marquee above reads, *"Fireworks Show Tonight!"* Max knocks on the ticket office door. Waits. No answer. He looks in, sees a desk with no one behind it. The place is empty.

Doyle rattles the doorknob and finds it locked, when record-breaking San Francisco Giant, Barry Bonds, rounds the corner.

Max jumps in front of him and quickly flashes his badge. "I'm Detective Lieutenant Max Tyrell. My partner and I are on a missing person's investigation."

Doyle, unwilling to wait, puts a rock through a pane of glass in the door. There's a loud crash, and the shrapnel covers the ground inside. He reaches in and unlocks the door. Max looks at Barry and shrugs. "Never mind." Barry shakes his head and moves along.

Broken glass crackles under their feet as they enter. The sound is shotgun loud in the quiet room. Max stands guard as Doyle rifles through short stacks of loose papers on the desk. He searches the drawers inside and pulls out a clipboard, studies it, and smiles. "Now, will the fish take the bait?" He picks up the phone, and dials.

Back at the Chimera compound, inside the first-floor office, boxes of cigarettes are stacked. A Chinese Clerk is at his laptop, paying Two Fingers and Hawk Eye for the voucher in $100 bills, bundled in red wrappers stamped "CHIMERA." Hawk Eye takes the incoming call on his mobile phone.

Through the phone, Doyle says, "Hawk Eye!"

"Doyle Donovan! You still alive?"

"I am. And thank you for asking." Doyle sits on the corner of the desk. "Now, would you be interested in the travel plans for a tractor trailer with ten tons of fireworks tonight?"

Hawk Eye is silent for a moment, considering the question. Then, "Okay. But when we split, we split my way. And no squawks. You get me?"

"Like a gallstone. I want twelve points for my tax."

"Six," Hawk Eye argues.

"Eight."

"Done," Hawk Eye says, rubbing his chin. "Now, where are these fireworks?"

TWENTY-SEVEN

JUST BEFORE DARK, inside Arlene's Truck Stop, people shovel down cups of bad coffee, plates of greasy burgers and aging pie. At the diesel pumps, a resting rig advertises *FIREWORKS! CAUTION: FIREWORKS! EXPLOSIVES!* on the side.

In the parking lot, Two Fingers and Hawk Eye sit in a Sedan, Two Fingers impatiently tapping on the steering wheel. Hawk Eye watches a man eat a burger through the window and wonders if the diner offers steak fries or thin cut.

"Wait until he finishes his dinner," Hawk Eye says. "Timing is everything." The man inside wipes his mouth and picks up the check. "And don't forget the kiddies."

Two Fingers nods, then reaches in the back seat and grabs a burlap sack. Something in the sack moves. Hawk Eye gets out of the car, and his friend follows. The two go around the invading lights at the gas pumps and stick to the shadows, then make a mad dash for the fireworks truck. Hawk Eye opens the driver's side door, and Two Fingers hands over the sack. "You sure they're harmless?" he asks.

"As dangerous as bunny rabbits." Hawk Eye takes the

sack and dumps the contents on the driver's seat. Gopher snakes slither from the bag and scatter throughout the truck's cab. "Unless one of 'em bites you."

They shut the door and scurry off behind a dumpster, where they anxiously wait for the trucker to discover their trap. They watch the man inside as he pays for his meal, grabs a toothpick from the holder next to the register, and walks out the door. He pulls a pack of smokes from his tight-fitting flannel and taps one out. Two Fingers quietly scratches paint from the side of the dumpster with his two fingers until Hawk Eye glares at him with his one good eye. Finally, the nail-biting moment arrives when the trucker gets to his rig, opens it, and climbs inside. The door shuts, and there's silence. No screaming. No shouting. No banging around. Nothing.

The engine starts.

Two Fingers nudges Hawk Eye. "What went wrong? Didn't it work?"

"Give it time," his partner says.

As though on cue, a muffled shriek comes from the cab, and the door flies open. The driver jumps out with snakes coiled around his neck, arm, and clasped in his hand. The man runs off into the darkness, hysterical.

○

Behind Chimera Dry Cleaners, Buzz Cut walks two women to the cleaning van. The two are dressed in low-cut, elastic dresses. One red, the other in black. While the dresses could pass for elegance, the garter belts state other-wise. These are clearly working girls.

Buzz Cut swings the van door open, and out pops Max by surprise, gun in his hand. "Get in the van," he says. Buzz

Cut throws his bandaged hands in the air, puts his head down, and complies.

Doyle eyes the two women, taking note of their bedroom garb. "We need to borrow your outfits, ladies."

The hookers look at Max and the gun in his hand, at Buzz Cut being forced into the van, and they start to strip down. While they undress, Doyle runs around the corner and comes back with Lydia Scarfoli and Emma Schlumburger. He gently helps each of them into the van, then offers a nod of gratitude at the hookers, takes their clothes, and climbs in himself. With a wave of the gun, Max tells Buzz Cut to step on it. Within seconds, they're on the road. Destination: San Jose.

With one hand holding on for balance at each turn, Lydia and Emma change into the hooker's clothes. They fit like well-worn gloves. Any tighter and the girl's would stop breathing.

Doyle sticks his head up front, where Max keeps his gun trained on the driver. "Remember yesterday at Scarfoli's?"

"I can't remember last night," Max says.

"Well... actually, that's probably a good thing. But, just in case anything happens to me..." Doyle reaches into his pocket and pulls out the $10,000 check Max had given to Scarfoli. "I wanted you to have this."

"What?! You're giving me back my own check? Ya swindler!" Max yanks the check free from Doyle's hand and stuffs it into his pocket.

Delgado drives down The Embarcadero, catching an occasional glimpse of the bay in between buildings, painted a cozy amber by the glow of distant bridge lights. On the car's dashboard, Delgado's mounted phone, the GPS tracking app blinking. It's following Max.

⛊

The fireworks rig rolls its eighteen wheels up to the Chimera compound. The horn blasts, and the sentry opens the entry gate. Wang Tzu waits inside the warehouse, as the truck pulls in, stops, and the engine dies. Two Fingers and Hawk Eye open the doors and step down from the giant truck, all snakes having been cleared from it.

"Hey, Wang Tzu!" Two Fingers gives a nod.

"The commode jockeys!" he replies. "What you got?"

Hawk Eye jerks his thumb toward the truck. "Can't you read?"

"I don't need toy explosives.

Two Fingers smiles. "The load's worth two hundred G's."

Wang Tzu studies the truck, reads the flashy font again as he walks alongside it. "I pay you twenty."

The two lackeys exchange frustrated glances. One sighs. The other shakes his head in disappointment, knowing it's the best deal they're going to get.

While the transaction is made, another guest pulls up to the compound gate–the dry cleaning van, with Buzz Cut at the wheel, packed with senior surprises, including two very scantily clad women. Without hesitation, the sentry opens the gate and waves the van in. Doyle hides further in the back, while Max ducks just behind the driver's seat, the Smith & Wesson still pointed at Buzz Cut. Buzz drives through the gate, and the sentry guards eye the female passengers, ogling them. Lydia and Emma hide their faces but allow their bulging bosoms to draw the sentries in.

The van pulls up behind a handful of workers

139

unloading a large crate of fireworks from the back of the semi. Another worker stands by with a dolly, ready to wheel the cargo away.

Max peeks out the windshield. "Park it here. By the fireworks."

Buzz Cut puts the van in park.

"Now, call those workers over here."

Buzz Cut rolls down the window, speaks in Chinese, "Hey, guys. Look what I brought."

The workers stop what they're doing and swivel their heads toward the van, then approach it. The van's back doors swing open, and out spill Lydia and Emma. Dresses tight as skin, makeup done to perfection, fake lashes batting. They wave fans and toss feather boas, concealing their wrinkled faces. The workers slither behind the van, darting their eyes back and forth between each set of breasts. The women work the men with moves they haven't used in years, a seducing dance honed in their prime.

While Chimera's employees are distracted, Max clocks Buzz Cut in the back of the head with the butt of the gun. The man's head bounces off the steering wheel, and the snoring begins. Doyle sneaks out the passenger door, and Max follows. Shadows in the darkened warehouse provide all the cover they need, as they bolt for a corner, round it, then head toward a row of lockers some twenty feet ahead.

Max opens one locker, Doyle another. Inside is workmen's gear—coveralls, caps, gloves, and paint masks. An entire ensemble to help with the success of the ruse.

"We have to work fast." Max puts a leg into the coveralls.

Doyle catches himself in a mirror stuck to the inside of the locker, notes the lipstick smudge on his face and wipes at it.

Max stops what he's doing and glares at his partner. "Faster."

TWENTY-EIGHT

AGENT QUICK WALKS into one of the more impressive rooms at the local headquarters for the Federal Bureau of Investigation. State-of-the-art satellite monitors and control consoles light up, and more agents pour in behind her like ants. They spread out, take their assigned stations, and await orders.

"It's show time!" Quick says, then presses a button on a nearby desk. "Red team. Report." She releases the button and waits.

Just outside the restrooms at San Francisco International, a man dressed in a janitor's uniform mops the floor in small, repetitive circles. His real focus is on Mr. Chan and the man's entourage who are going through customs after having just landed in Chimera's private jet.

The janitor lifts an arm and discreetly speaks into the cuff of his shirt sleeve. "Our package has cleared customs."

Agent Quick is now in transit, sitting in the back seat of

a black SUV while another agent drives. She speaks into her own communicator, "Blue team report."

Two blocks from the Chimera compound, a telephone repairman stands at the back of his open work van. With eyes on a black Bentley Mulsanne, he speaks into his wrist. "The package is being delivered."

The Bentley, bearing the Chimera symbol on its side, pulls up to the security gate at the compound. The armed sentries peek at the passengers inside, then wave it in.

Arriving at their destination, Agent Quick's driver parks at the top of a tall hill overlooking the compound. Agent Quick steps out of the SUV and puts a pair of binoculars to her face. The driving agent, dressed in a black suit, gets out and stands next to her, arms crossed.

"Call in tactical," Quick says.

From inside headquarters, FBI dispatchers receive the message. A woman behind the computer types frantically but precise, getting the word out. Others send texts. And one speaks into a cellphone, relaying the message. "FBI SWAT, be advised. This is a Level Five warning. Immediate need for overwhelming force—"

Lydia and Emma continue their burlesque dance, still hiding their faces with large, paper fans, which they now incorporate into the dance. Every man in the warehouse stops what they're doing and watches on, catcalling, whistling.

Elsewhere in the warehouse, now fully dressed in a Chimera jumpsuit and paint mask, Max points out Xhing to Doyle. "Check out King Kong over there. Tattooed scalp and all."

Xhing opens the second-floor loft door to his office and

heads inside. Only a brief moment passes before Wang Tzu exits the room, followed by Xhing who drags an exhausted and frightened couple along with him. It's Susan and Cosmo. All four walk down the stairs, and Cosmo's eyes go wide as he makes eye contact with his father. An attentive Xhing spots the change in Cosmo's face and follows his line of sight, straight to Doyle and the rage-filled determination in his face. With the couple in his grasp, Xhing dips away through rows of pallets and cardboard boxes.

Near the delivery van, Hawk Eye and Two Fingers join the lust-filled audience, getting an eyeful of leg and cleavage. The Bentley pulls up next to them and parks. The door opens, and out steps Mr. Chan.

"Welcome to America, Boss," Wang Tzu says.

Mr. Chan pays no mind to the entertainment and brushes lint from his sleeve. "Everything ready?"

"Yes."

The ladies continue their dance, providing more than adequate distraction, while Max and Doyle sneak into the fireworks trailer, dressed in full Chimera attire. Once inside, Max strikes a match and holds it to the cigar jutting from his mouth. He puffs until there's a healthy ember stoked at the end.

Doyle looks around at the tightly stacked boxes of fireworks and panics. "Are you crazy? You wanna smoke in here?"

"It's a fuse." Max speaks out the side of his mouth. "Gives us some time to get away. This thing blows, you don't wanna be around."

Doyle looks at him dumbfounded. "You think this rescue's going well?"

"Better than some..." Max bites off the wet end of the cigar, spits it out, and gently sets the fuse in place atop a case of tightly packaged Roman candles. He gives a thumbs up, and the two turn to exit the trailer, when Wang Tzu and Xhing appear before them, blocking their exit. "...but not as well as others."

Doyle looks terrified, unsure of what to do, and turns to Max.

"Never too early to panic," Max says, then draws his gun. But Xhing sees the move coming and stops Max with a hard backhand to the face, dropping the older man to the hard, wooden floor of the rig's trailer. The gun leaves Max's hand and slides away. He reaches for it, willing his fingers to stretch another inch, but Wang Tzu retrieves the pistol and nods at Xhing. The ape responds to the command by giving Max a swift punch to the kidneys, then dragging him out of the trailer by his collar.

The fight for freedom is short, and the ineffective heroes are hauled away, bruised and bleeding.

TWENTY-NINE

DEEP INSIDE THE WAREHOUSE, a table sits in the middle of a large room. Max and Doyle hang nearby, suspended by their wrists from the emergency sprinkler system. Face-to-face. Blackened eyes and bloodied noses.

"For sixteen years, I've hated you." Max says, his face stretched into a mask of pain and disgust. "Now the last thing I get to see is your ugly face. It ain't right."

Doyle closes his eyes. His lips move, but no sound passes through them.

Max scrunches his face. "What are you doing?"

"Praying. For a miracle."

"*Now* you got religion?"

〇

Elsewhere in the warehouse, Susan and Cosmo sit inside the first-floor office, bound to chairs. Cosmo's eyes are both blackened, his upper lip caked with drying blood. Susan's cheek is bright red, a split bottom lip packed with congealment, her mouth gagged with a bandana. She kicks out at Xhing, and he slaps her. Again.

The door opens, and in walks Mr. Chan. Immaculate suit. Not a hair out of place. Manicured nails. He looks at Cosmo. "I need you to sign these." Opens the briefcase in his hand, takes out a short stack of papers, uncaps an ink pen, and writes his own signature a dozen times, on as many pages.

"You're wasting your time," Cosmo tells him.

Wang Tzu gives Xhing a signal by way of a nod, and Xhing punches Cosmo in the face. His head snaps back, and the blood flows again. Susan belts out a muffled scream and kicks out again, as she struggles against the restraints wrapped around her and the chair. Making sure the message is getting across, Xhing throws another punch, nearly knocking Cosmo and his chair over. Mr. Chan holds his hand up, signaling Xhing to stop. Xhing complies, and the grin on his face says he's more than willing to continue, just give the signal.

Cosmo spits blood. "You can't just take my life's work."

Mr. Chan kneels down, meeting Cosmo eye to eye. "Oh, but I can."

○

Max twists in the air, struggling to bring his feet up near his hands. Up, up near the sprinkler. It's a pointless endeavor. He rests his head on his chest and lets out a sigh, then looks at Doyle with an idea. "Get my knife. It's in my boot."

"Sure thing," Doyle says. "I'll just reach down there and get it real quick. Need anything else while I'm down there? Maybe a foot massage? I could order some take out, make a night of it."

Max looks up and tries to nod at the sprinkler above him. "Just swing! Swing and hook your feet on the sprinkler, then unhook your hands and you can reach my boot."

Doyle studies the sprinkler and notes he actually would be able to free his hands if he could somehow manage to get his feet up there. So, with zero expectation, he makes the effort and starts to rock, building momentum. The effort stops when the table below catches his eye. There's something on it he hadn't noticed before. Stacks upon stacks of the counterfeit money.

"Well, would you look at all that."

Max huffs and rolls his eyes. "I've got to hand it to you, Doyle. You don't stop." He shakes his head in disgust. "I should have never listened to you. I knew better than to give you the time of day. 'It's a fortress,' I said. 'Sit there and admire me for a while. I just got an idea for a plan,' you said."

Doyle starts to swing again and bumps into Max, "I said– ?"

Max groans at the collision. "Have the police storm a compound? What could go wrong?', you said. Ha! 'This'll have to be a SWAT callout,' I said. 'Did you forget what happened in Waco?', you said." Max braces for impact again, squints his eyes.

"I said–?" Doyle swings higher. Harder.

"And Ruby Ridge–?" Doyle bumps Max harder this time, accidentally poking his knee into Max's gut, knocking the last few words out of him.

"Our kids are in here! Besides..." Doyle swings towards Max again, nearly there with his feet. "...look at all that money we've found."

"You know what kills me?" Max says.

"What's'a matter?" Doyle grunts through the words.

"You never listen to me! And look where we are now..."

Finally, Doyle's feet swing high and hook onto the sprinkler holding Max's hands. He lifts his tied hands up and over the sprinkler, and his upper body drops. The momentum slams Doyle's face into Max, but this time it's a face-to-crotch meeting.

"Ow!" Doyle yells. "You tryin' to poke my eye out with that thing? Next time, just one Viagra, stud."

"Can it, and get my knife."

Like the world's largest geriatric bat, Doyle hangs upside down, his feet now held by the same sprinkler head that Max dangles from. He stretches his arms out as far as he can but can't quite make it to his partner's boots. "A little help here?"

Max lifts his leg holding the knife and knocks his knee into the top of Doyle's head. A two-man choir of pain-filled groans fill the room. The two shake it off and try again. This time, Doyle grabs hold of Max's boot and slips a thumb and forefinger inside. He feels for the knife, finds it, pulls it out. "Got it!" He keeps hold of the leg and uses Max's body to climb back up, resting his butt on Max's shoulders.

"Don't drop it," Max says, turning his face away from Doyle's intruding rear end. "Hurry up."

Doyle saws through the ropes that bind his own feet, as well as Max's hands. The threads are severed, and they brace for impact. For a two-foot drop, the crash is hard, especially for Max, who lands first and breaks Doyle's fall.

Max shoves his partner off him and grabs the knife from his hand. He cuts through the rope around his ankles, then around Doyle's wrists. As they struggle to their feet, Doyle pauses, fixated on the table and its stacked contents a mere ten feet away.

"Doyle? No! Don't even think about it. That's monopoly money. Now, c'mon." Max sticks his knife back in his boot.

"There must be over half a million dollars sitting there." Doyle takes out his phone.

"What're you doing?"

"Calling for backup."

"*Now* you wanna call the cops?!"

"Not that kind of backup, Clouseau. I'm callin' in a marker."

○

Susan and Cosmo sit bound to their chairs in the downstairs office, when the door opens. In walks Xhing, with a frightened Talulah in his grip.

"Mom! Dad!" Talulah tries to run to her parents, but Xhing pulls her back. She kicks at his shins, but he picks her up and ties a rope around her, cinching her arms to her ribs and her ankles together.

Susan's eyes go wild, as she screams behind the gag, struggling more than ever against the restraints that hold her to the chair—a mother's instinct at its most primal stage.

"Please. Let her go," Cosmo pleads.

Mr. Chan steps forward, points behind him to the stack of papers on the large, metal desk. "Your choice is simple. You both sign this agreement. Or... you both watch me kill your daughter. Very slowly."

○

Max and Doyle exit the second-floor loft office and race down the balcony. No time to be stealthy. Before they reach the stairs, three of Xhing's guards appear, advancing towards them. Muscle packed inside yard-sale suits.

"Let's take 'em, Tonto!" Max reaches out and grabs Doyle's hand, forming a flying wedge as they bolt toward the guards. The muscle-bound men brace themselves but underestimate the older men and are thrown backward down the metal stairs.

Agent Quick, still on the hill, watches Delgado through the binoculars, who sits in his unmarked Sedan at the entry gate to Chimera, fingers frantically tapping the steering wheel.

"You can take your tin badges and stick 'em where the sun don't shine." Delgado is saying to one of the sentries at the gate. "I've got backup coming. SFPD SWAT will be here any second. I'm just waitin' on them."

Behind Quick, FBI SWAT teams pour from buses, securing their bulletproof vests, double checking ammunition. Every one of them is armed and dangerous to any criminal in their way.

Quick's eyes stay glued to the interaction at the gate. "We have a party crasher."

In the dry-cleaning van, Buzz Cut peels his lids open and regains consciousness. Woozy, he rubs the goose egg on his head and quietly moans. Nearby, Lydia and Emma dance, their audience still captivated, although Hawk Eye begins to scrutinize them, suspicious of their age and why they're here.

Inside the fireworks truck, Max's cigar fuse has burnt almost all the way down, while the charred hole under it continues to burn through the package, nearing the now exposed Roman candles.

Cosmo stands at the desk with pen in hand, his shirt stained with blood. He leans over the desk, ready to sign the contract given him by Chan, giving up all rights to his life-changing invention, placing everything he's worked for into the hands of a ruthless criminal. The pen touches paper, and an explosion shakes the building.

From the hill, Agent Quick watches a portion of the warehouse's roof blow open. The fireworks rig brings the dark night to life, emitting an intense shower of sparks and multi-colored fire, sending everyone near to scatter for their lives. Through the binoculars, Quick zeroes in on Delgado's Sedan, as the Lieutenant's car races forward and smashes through the entry gate.

She pulls the binocs away. "Let's roll." The SWAT team behind her springs into action. Vehicle doors slam, engines come to life, and the convoy heads out, with all wheels racing for the Chimera compound.

Smoke fills the compound, as Max and Doyle run aimlessly through the warehouse. A woman's shrill scream gives them pause, and they change direction, heading toward the panic-filled voice. The smoke screen temporarily thins, and Doyle spots Lydia and Emma, hands clasped together and lost in the smoke. He calls out to them, and Lydia turns to him.

Placing a hand to her heart, she calls back to him, "Il mio eroe!"

Hurriedly, he waves them over, and the women sprint toward him.

"Here. Grab some of these." Max points to an open crate of fireworks.

The women grab a handful of cherry bombs and roman candles and shove them into the tops of their dresses, where they rest outlined in the stretchy fabric. After loading up on the tiny explosives, they all run to the first-floor office, where the blinds are drawn, blocking any sight of those inside. Max nods at the women, and Emma pulls a firecracker from her top. She holds it out for Lydia, who hurries with the lighter, sparks a flame, and holds it to the small bomb's wick. It catches, hisses, and Emma tosses the bomb at the office door, quickly followed by another.

Doyle cups his hands and yells at the door. "Run for your lives! Everybody out now! This place is coming down!"

The door flies open and out runs Mr. Chan, who jumps at a cherry bomb exploding at his feet.

"Eh, stronzo!" Lydia calls out from behind a tall stack of pallets, while lighting the roman candle in Emma's hand. The candle fires off, and the first bang explodes against Chan's rear end. He spins around to face her.

Emma says, "We've got something for you, bless your heart!"

Lydia pitches a lit cherry bomb at Chan's face. It hits its target and explodes. Chan screams, shouting a string of threats, while Max rushes past him and darts into the office.

☖

Fireworks of varying degree continue to shoot from the truck's trailer. Some shoot skyward, some zoom horizontally, all of them ending in an explosive bang.

The smoke thickens, and a cacophony of symphonic chaos echoes through the warehouse, as sirens and flashing lights outside lead the convoy of FBI SWAT through the destroyed gate and into the compound.

A wide-eyed sentry makes an urgent call on his radio, warning everyone, "The outer perimeter has been broken!"

Cardboard boxes throughout the warehouse have created a spreading fire, and the emergency sprinklers begin their prompted shower in a pathetic attempt at counterattacking the growing flames.

Chimera guards aim their automatic weapons from behind parked vehicles and cement walls, peppering the FBI SWAT with bullets. Without hesitation, SWAT fires back. At least a dozen workers inside flee the scene, scattering in as many directions. Some run deeper into the warehouse, further into the walls of smoke in order to distance themselves from gunfire. Others run outside, taking their chances against SWAT or outgoing crossfire, most of them with arms in the air in a pose of surrender.

Buzz Cut runs from the van, pushing through the smoke and confusion, running with his head ducked and coughing through the toxic smoke, doing his best to dodge the bullets.

◯

The first-floor office is filling with smoke when Max enters. The room is large enough for him to initially go unnoticed, while Xhing and Wang Tzu peek through the blinds, watching the fire grow and deciding their next move. Max doesn't see Talulah or Susan right away but does spot Cosmo and goes for the rope around his wrists. He rips through them with the knife, when movement elsewhere catches his eye. Talulah, securely bound and struggling against the restraints. His eyes then shift to Xhing, and he puts a hand on Cosmo's shoulder. Just above a whisper,

154

"Step aside, Scooter. Youth is great, but it's no match for old age."

"Where are you going?" Cosmo asks.

"To beat the living crap out of a dirt bag."

It takes two seconds for Max to get to the far side of the room, where he throws a right and connects with an unexpecting Xhing. The ape responds with a wide grin and a powerfully quick haymaker. Max takes the hit and falls back onto Cosmo's skateboard nearby.

With a pop of his knee, he stands back up and taps the tale of the board with his foot. The thing flips up and into hands. It's a weapon now. Max swings the seven-ply board and whacks Xhing hard in the face. The man drops to his knees, momentarily dazed.

"Well, whaddaya know?" Max looks at Cosmo, stands triumphantly over his opponent, with skateboard in hand. "This thing's good for somethin' after all."

Behind Max, Wang Tzu draws his gun and aims it, finger on the trigger and ready to pull, when Doyle suddenly appears through the smoke. His fist splits the air and smashes into Wang Tzu's eye, spinning him around. The gun's trigger is pulled, and the shot goes wild, burying itself in the wall.

"Dad?!" Cosmo taken by complete surprise, finishes what his father started, by boxing Wang Tzu's ears, kicking him in the crotch, and spinning him back around, finally causing the man to drop the gun.

"I know why they snatched Talulah. You should've come to me." Doyle grabs a fire extinguisher propped on the wall and cracks Wang Tzu in the head with it. *Conk!*

"They said they'd kill everybody if I told anyone."

"Son, I'm not just anyone."

Flames infiltrate the room, reaching for anything that will allow the spreading of its growing heat, licking at cardboard, paneling, and even the ceiling. Xhing shakes the woozy out of his head and grins at Max. He scrambles to his feet and draws a large commando knife, reels it back and lumbers toward Max, who takes aim with Wang Tzu's gun and fires.

Click!

The gun is empty.

Cosmo shouts to Max, "Hand me my board!"

Max looks down, sees he still holds the skateboard in his left hand, and hands it over. Cosmo steps in front of Max, drops the board and steps on it, while Xhing inches closer with the knife.

Max reaches out and snatches Cosmo's arm. "Where do you think you're going?"

"Stay out of my way, Gramps. I don't want you getting hurt."

Cosmo puts his foot down and pushes off, leaving behind a grumbling Max. "Gramps? Hurt?!"

Before Cosmo gets to Xhing, he ollies up and over him, while keeping hold of the deck. Xhing's knife slashes the empty air, and Cosmo lands expertly. He turns 180 degrees on his tail and pushes off, back toward Xhing. But Xhing is ready this time and throws his arm out, catching Cosmo before he can land the trick. The board crashes to the floor, and so does Cosmo.

Max grabs his knife from his boot, and jumps in between Xhing and Cosmo. It's a close-quarters knife fight, between the desk and the wall. Arms swing, slicing the air between them, but no purchase is made.

While Max is busy, Doyle runs to the other side of the room and frees Susan from the binding ropes.

Xhing swings, then thrusts, and Max grabs his arm. He quickly wraps his tie around the man's knife with the hope of hindering further use of the weapon, but Xhing cuts right through.

"Hey! I went to my daughter's graduation in that tie!"

While running his mouth, Max doesn't see Xhing's backhand coming, until it hits his wrist, throwing the knife from his hand. The knife lands on the desk behind him, and Xhing swings out again. Max backs up and gropes for his knife, but only finds a nearby laptop. Out of desperation, he grabs it and blocks the next swing. A quick shove, and Max is able to swing the computer, using it as a weapon. Xhing's head takes the first hit, and the ape stumbles back. Max goes in with another try and connects yet again. And again. But Xhing chuckles, unfazed, and raises his knife.

The glint of the blade catches in Max's wide eyes. And before the blade comes down, he holds the laptop as a shield. The knife comes down with force and slides through the makeshift shield. The momentum rips the computer from Max's hands and crashes to the floor, while the knife remains through it, blade side up.

Xhing wastes no time in continuing his attack on the defenseless Max, by putting him in a chokehold, while the heat in the room rises to near unbearable levels. Max grunts through it, and manages to throw a vicious right cross into the chinaman's jaw.

From the far side of the room, Cosmo jumps back on the board, pushes off, and ollies over the desk. The only landing zone is Xhing. The skateboard crashes into his side. Ribs crack and knees buckle, sending him backward onto the laptop and creating a human kebob, as the knife through the computer punctures his back.

Max quickly crawls over. "Wait! My first aid training said direct pressure is the best treatment for heavy bleeding." He falls on top of Xhing, putting both hands on his chest, and pushing down, impaling the man further onto his own knife, while the room fills with a groaning scream.

Buzz Cut, alerted by Xhing's cry of pain, appears in the doorway behind Max. He pulls a gun from his side and aims. "Say goodbye, old man!"

From outside the room, Delgado charges. "You're under arr–." A full body tackle into Buzz Cut takes him down, and a bullet fires from the gun. Another wild miss.

With Buzz Cut out cold, Delgado checks on Max, who has since rolled off from Xhing and is lying by his side, eyes closed, catching his breath. Delgado looks down. "Did King Kong hurt you?"

Max's eyes flutter open, takes a moment to focus on Delgado. "I'm not hurt."

Delgado reaches down and lends him a hand. Max takes it. "Okay... I'm a little banged up." He gets a look at the growing fire. Inferno levels. "Let's go!" He ushers his daughter and Talulah out of the office, as the ceiling behind them collapses, burying Xhing and Buzz Cut under its smoldering debris.

Doyle escorts his son, and they march through the obstructing smoke, following Delgado's lead to safety. Through the smoke, they can see SWAT has arrived, while more of their motorcade race through the leveled gate, but the barrage of bullets from both sides shut down the idea that outside is any safer than in, as the constant explosion of gunfire adds to the chorus of fireworks, making it difficult to tell the difference between the two.

Warehouse workers continue to run aimlessly through the smoke, scurrying off in random directions. Screaming, shouting, every one of them terrified of either dying or prison.

Near the warehouse entrance, Two Fingers and Hawk Eye tip over old merchandise racks, piling them as a defensive perimeter, then sprint to an overturned table for cover. Bullets spray the table top, splintering the wood and bending the hardware.

Cosmo drops his board, hops on, and pushes off, drawing gunfire from Chan's men. Carving and sliding, he dodges the rain of bullets. He ollies, does a wall ride up and over a stack of boxes, lands, then ollies again, while the microchip in the board offers the precise speed and balance needed with each land, allowing an almost inhuman ability to dodge the incessant gunfire. He's an absolute blur to anyone taking aim.

Outside, the SFPD SWAT pushes, doubling down with the bullets, tossing in flash bombs and tear gas grenades.

Some twenty feet away, a smoldering man holds a gun with Max in its sights. Buzz Cut has found a way out of the collapsed room, his face raw with burns, hair singed away. But before the trigger is pulled, Cosmo sails through the air, and Buzz takes a tail to the face. Once again Cosmo lands with perfection, while the burned man drops to the ground in a heap.

With no idea he'd nearly lost his head, Max swings a lead pipe at a guard, and it's lights out for the Chimera employee. Max takes the man's gun and sees another guard attempting to hide behind a stack of boxes while loading a pistol. Max takes aim, squints. It's no good. He pats his pockets down for Doyle's glasses. Finds them, puts them on. Much better. After careful aim, the villain goes down.

Two Fingers and Hawk Eye cower at the relentless onslaught of SWAT bullets, leaving their position behind the table that's become nothing but splintered shards of its former self, and run for refuge among a row of boxes.

A guard raises his weapon, and yet another gun is aimed at Max while he's a sitting duck. But the sound of polyurethane wheels spinning on pavement grows closer to the guard, as Cosmo saves the day again. This time Cosmo jumps off of the board and gives the guard a swift kick to the head. Another tucked in for the night, then Cosmo hops back on and takes off toward the others.

Emma spots an AK-47 clutched in the hands of a downed guard and grabs it. She tosses the gun to Cosmo as he rides by. He catches the AK and does a one-eighty. The board's wheels screech against the floor, and he pulls the gun's trigger. The recoil pushes him, and now he's riding backward, as the bullets head toward more of Chimera's guards.

The guards fire back. Cosmo dodges, and Max leaps out of line of fire, while SWAT keeps at it. Stray bullets *tink*, bounce, and bury, as people cower and run. Max peeks out from behind a corner, takes aim at one of Chimera's guard. He fires, and the guard collapses. He aims again at another.

Click! Empty. Deja Vu.

Max takes cover, while Buzz Cut gets back on his feet, refusing to stay down. Wang Tzu and he reload their own guns, then fire rapid shots. One points in Max's direction, the other toward SWAT.

With nowhere else to go, Hawk Eye and Two Fingers find themselves cornered where the fire is hottest. Sweat drips, eyes widen, and prayers are spoken. Looks like the end of the line.

A SWAT officer speaks through a bullhorn: "Drop your weapons, and put your hands over your heads!"

All shooting ceases, and dust settles. Even the fireworks die down, though the fire rages on, slowing consuming the warehouse. Firetrucks break the brief moment of silence, as their sirens scream onto the compound. Readied men jump from the trucks, preparing for battle against the flames.

Somewhere in the back, an explosion, and another

ceiling collapses. Emma and Lydia drop their guns and throw their hands in the air, while heading toward SWAT.

"Che macello!" Lydia says.

The remaining guards alive comply with SWAT and slowly walk out, coughing into the increasingly smokey air. Two Fingers and Hawk Eye find themselves doing the same, defeated and scared.

The SFPD SWAT swarm like flies, apprehending Wang Tzu's men, handcuffing them, then herding them into SF Police Department vans.

Doyle escorts an exhausted Emma and Lydia—one on each arm—past Hawk Eye and Two Fingers. "You owe me eight points for the tax on the fireworks, Hawk Eye."

Hawk Eye snarls his lip. "And if you ever wanna see it, go make yourself useful and—"

"—and call that slimeball lawyer of yours for us." Two Fingers spins his wrists against the cuffs around them.

A gurney is loaded into an ambulance. It's Xhing, face down, a knifed laptop stuck through the ribs in his back. The man moans as the gurney bounces and is fed into the back of the vehicle.

Agent Quick stands with her gun pointed at Wang Tzu himself. He's on his knees, both hands over his head. She leans in, stares down the sights of her gun. "You won't be needing this where you're going." Quick snatches Wang Tzu's gun from out of his hand, then turns to the uniforms beside her. "Get this sack of shit out of my sight."

Talulah tackles Doyle and Max together, bringing them into a hug. She's sobbing. "I was so scared. My grandpops!" She can barely get the next few words out. "I love you both so much!"

Max revels in the moment. It's a moment he wasn't sure would ever happen, and to feel the thin arm of his grand-daughter hold him so tight, trembling with joy of her own.

Not even Doyle as part of the group hug can ruin a time like this. And yes, he supposes her other grandpop deserves the same love. He was, as much as Max hates to admit it, of some use in the rescue, even a good... *partner.*

They all make their way to Susan, who sits on the back of an ambulance, being checked over by a first responder. Max reaches a hand out and grabs hers. "Susan... are you alright?" She wraps her arms around her father, reaching for Doyle and pulling him in. Another group hug. Still doesn't ruin the moment. She squeezes them and gives them both a kiss on the check. Her smile is ear to ear. "I'm fine, Dad. We're all fine."

Max looks over and feels a great warmth in his heart as he catches a glimpse of his granddaughter hugging her father—a touching reunion.

Doyle sees Wang Tzu on his knees and being cuffed. He heads over, just long enough to put a bug in the villain's ear. "When you get out of prison, you'll be my age. It's all over, moron."

Two policeman pull Wang Tzu to his feet, and rage-filled blood rushes to his face. He takes in a deep breath and grits his teeth. "Jail in your country is a vacation. I'm the most dangerous man in the world. I can still get you and your precious granddaughter... even from behind bars. God bless America."

Lieutenant Delgado looks to Agent Quick, who now has a handcuffed Mr. Chan in her grasp. "Well... what're you gonna do about that?"

Quick shrugs her shoulders. "I just collared the counterfeit ring king. I got what I was after." She nods to Wang Tzu. "That lowlife is your problem."

Delgado then turns to Doyle. "The most dangerous man in the world says he's still a threat."

"And that's why he's a moron," Doyle says.

The policemen drag away Wang Tzu. Lydia Scarfoli gives Doyle a knowing nod as they pass by, noting one of the "policemen" wears alligator skin boots with shiny studs on the toes. Doyle grins back at Lydia, then sidles up to Max. "We did it... Partner."

It's true. There's no denying it. Max gives in and offers his hand. They shake, and it morphs into a hug. "We sure did," he says, then holds Doyle shoulders at arm's length and throws an arm around Cosmo. "But... this is my new partner." Max pulls him in and squeezes. "You did all right, Scooter!"

Cosmo smiles and locks eyes with Susan.

"Go ahead. Ask him," she says.

Cosmo pauses, clears his throat, and turns to Max. He takes a deep breath. "Does this mean you'll finally give us your sacred blessing?"

THIRTY

MAX STANDS OUTSIDE ST. Jude's Church. He's clean shaven, dressed in a dark suit. Father O'Brian stands next to him, discussing the recent harrowing events, as guests pass by and enter the church for the upcoming wedding ceremony inside.

"You mean the biggest counterfeiter in the world was trying to steal the patent on your future, good-for-nothing son-in-law's multi-billion-dollar skateboard invention?" Father O'Brian says.

Max lights his cigar, puffs on it. "Maybe I got the kid all wrong."

Oscar, the man who oversees the office at Paradise Village, steps up to Max. "Your credit check cleared. Here ya go." Through a handshake, he offers Max a set of room keys.

Max nods at the man. "Thanks, Oscar."

◌

Inside the church, Ursula from the skate shop, helps Susan with her wedding gown, tugging and smoothing out the

164

white, elegant silk. Susan beams as she looks at herself in the mirror. She's a bride. Finally!

Doyle, dressed to please in his Sunday's best, watches from the other side of the room, wearing his own prideful smile that hasn't left all morning. He leans over and gives Talulah a tight, one-armed hug, then hands her a basket of flowers.

Max heads inside this sixty-seat church through the double doors that have been propped open. He walks through the vestibule and opens the door to the chapel. Pokes his head in. The groom's side is packed, every seat with someone anxiously waiting. On the bride's side is Ira, the only one there for Max, in his wheelchair, with his oxygen tank. The father of the bride frowns, lets out a sigh with a shake of his head, and closes the door.

Delgado shows up, decked out in a crisp, blue uniform. Newly ironed, adorned with all the appropriate medals for a lieutenant in the field. He greets Max with a hearty handshake. "Max. Your big day. How's it feel–?"

In the street, the brakes of a yellow school bus hiss as the bus pulls up in front of St. Jude's. The doors open, and a couple dozen young adults file out, heading toward the church.

Ursula gives one last tug on Susan's dress. "Looks like your friends just got here."

Susan looks through the window. "I don't know any of these people."

"Not my tribe," Doyle says.

Talulah peeks, then shrugs. "Don't look at me."

Max spots the brand new captain's bars on Delgado's uniform. He smiles, pretends to dust off the adornment. "Congratulations, *Captain*. You didn't wait for backup."

The busload of people make their way through the

vestibule, as Delgado pats Max on the shoulder. "They tell you don't ever go in by yourself. But, if you do…"

The people stand behind Max, silent. Max turns and sees a young man in his twenties at the head of the line. There's a smile on the man's face, but it's smothered, like he's trying to hide it. "Detective Tyrell… we know you got in trouble for saving our lives that day… on the bus, when we were in grade school." The man points a thumb at the bus outside. "And we wanted to thank you for that. And to be with you today, to celebrate with you. To make sure you'll never be alone."

Max's eyes go glassy, and his lips tighten. Each person in line takes their turn hugging a shaken Max, thanking him personally. Thirty-plus hugs later, they all enter the chapel and take a seat on the bride's side, with one left standing now that Max's side has filled.

"It's a wonderful life…" Doyle squeezes Max's shoulder, "…Partner."

Delgado nods in agreement, then pats Doyle on the arm. "Hey, Doyle. That 'moron,' Wang Tzu, is MIA. Since we're in church, you got anything you wanna confess?"

Doyle looks around suspiciously. "Can you keep a secret?"

Delgado leans in. "Of course I can keep a secret."

Doyle offers a toothy grin. "Good. So can I."

○

Inside the Scarfoli Funeral Parlor's embalming room, Wang Tzu lies strapped to a table, a hanging bag of fluid next to him, the connected IV tube taped to his arm. "Who are you?" he asks the woman in the room. "Why are you doing this?"

Lydia Scarfoli pets her new cat. "Ma dai! Doyle is calling in his marker."

Fugazzi leans in, trying to hold back a fit of nervous giggling. "He must really hate you."

Nick Scarfoli reaches for the button on the embalming machine, and Wang Tzu's eyes fixate on the button, his face stricken with fear. "Name your price!" he pleads.

"This isn't about money."

"Then what do you want?" Sweat beads on his forehead.

"I promised Doyle we'd embalm you while you're still breathing." The cat stretches, pushing up into Lydia's hand.

"Please! Don't do this. I've learned my lesson!"

Lydia's brow comes together with sinister intent. "Ti sta bene!" She nods, then Nick pushes the button, and the cat pounces onto Wang Tzu's face. He screams in pain-filled agony, while Fugazzi watches, giggling into his hand.

◯

Shafts of sunlight bring the chapel to life, as people finish taking their seats. Murmuring voices cease as organ music fills the room. The doors to the chapel fly open with a burst of energy. Talulah enters first. The flower girl. She carries a wicker basket full of pink and red rose petals, periodically tossing them to the floor. Next is Doyle, Ursula in his arm. Then Max with his daughter. The bride, illuminating. All eyes are on her.

She leans into her father. "This is the happiest day of my life."

"Then why spoil it with a wedding?" Max cracks a smile.

She pinches the underside of his arm, and he quietly squeals. "Don't start, Dad."

They join Father O'Brian, Cosmo, Doyle, and Ursula at the altar. Max lets go of his daughter and stands alongside Doyle, getting a good look at the groom's side chapel: The skaters, the Scarfolis. Oscar, Emma. Rosie and her crew. And all the men after Doyle.

Max slowly looks at Doyle, whispers, "Why don't these bruisers want to kill you anymore? Some kinda code of honor among criminals?"

"Just paid everyone off, is all."

"How did you–" He stops, reflects. "Doyle! You didn't go back for that monopoly money, did you?"

Doyle's eye seems to light up as he offers a quick wink. Aghast, Max steps back, and his knee pops. "Jesus H–!"

The music cuts, and the church fills with the echo of Father O'Brian's reprimand. "Maaaaax!"

Max rubs his knee. "Sorry, Father. I've really been trying hard to stop swearing."

"Try harder!"